FABLE
HOUSE

FABLE HOUSE

E.L. NORRY

BLOOMSBURY
CHILDREN'S BOOKS
LONDON OXFORD NEW YORK NEW DELHI SYDNEY

BLOOMSBURY CHILDREN'S BOOKS
Bloomsbury Publishing Plc
50 Bedford Square, London WC1B 3DP, UK
29 Earlsfort Terrace, Dublin 2, Ireland

BLOOMSBURY, BLOOMSBURY CHILDREN'S BOOKS and the
Diana logo are trademarks of Bloomsbury Publishing Plc

First published in Great Britain in 2023 by Bloomsbury Publishing Plc

A catalogue record for this book is available from the British Library

ISBN: PB: 978-1-5266-4953-9; eBook: 978-1-5266-4952-2;
ePDF: 978-1-5266-4951-5

2 4 6 8 10 9 7 5 3 1

Typeset by RefineCatch Limited, Bungay, Suffolk
Printed and bound in Great Britain by CPI Group (UK) Ltd, Croydon CR0 4YY

To find out more about our authors and books visit www.bloomsbury.com
and sign up for our newsletters

Welcome. This book is for you.
Heather, Lloyd, Arlene and Nat live in my heart.
I hope they find a place in yours

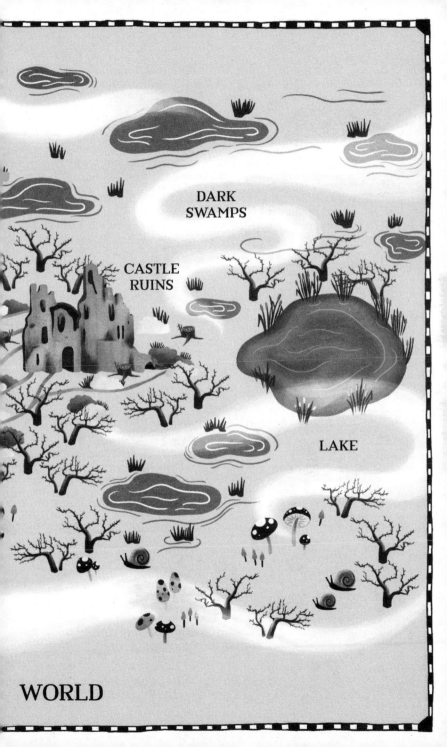

Chapter One

The Cairn

June 1954

'Gerroff me!'

Hurtling forward, away from Miss Gloria and her dreaded metal comb, I pushed past Judy, playing with her dolls, and dashed out of the common room.

I bounded up the rickety wooden stairs two at a time, up three flights, almost to the attic, which used to be the old servants' quarters. Hands on my knees, I crouched and took great gulping breaths while my heartbeat slowed. Even though I was out of sight, Miss Gloria still hollered my name from downstairs.

'HEATHER!'

I knew she wasn't really cross, but there was no way I was gonna let her get anywhere near me with that comb neither. Not if she knew what was good for her.

'Where's that Heather's got to?'

Miss Gloria was seventeen, and one of the staff who watched over us children here at Fablehouse. She loved combing our hair and fussing over our pinafores, like we were her own real-life dolls.

When I'd arrived a week before, she'd rattled on about being clean, tidy and 'respectable' – said it was expected of 'young ladies'. But my hair don't need brushing every day – what a waste of time that'd be! Fixing my fuzzball with a fat rubber band would do me just fine. Then at my weekly bathtime I could just sink under the water and let the soapy suds clean my curls. There wasn't any need to mess about with plaits and bunches and whatnot. And since when did looking 'nice' mean diddly-squat? It wasn't as if people would line up to adopt me anyway. I couldn't see how this place would be any different from the other homes I'd been in.

'Heather! Sweetie! Come on now.' Even far away as I was, her voice still echoed through corridors. I crept along the back hallways and nipped down the old servants' staircase that no one seemed to use, probably because it was riddled with woodworm and spiderwebs.

I was aiming for the back door as the ghostly echoes of 'Be a good girl and come on down here! Why you always running away?' followed me.

Miss Gloria was so smiley – weren't natural to be that cheerful. That entire week, I never saw her get annoyed or raise her hand, not even to the younger ones, and they whined something chronic. But no one's made of rainbows right through, are they? I reckoned that's why she liked doing our hair so much; that was how she got her anger out – by yanking and pulling at our knots and curls. And with thirteen of us, all with frizzy curly hair, there was definitely enough tangles to go around.

She always beamed when she was done too, sounding so satisfied.

'See? There. Much better, don't you think?' she'd said the other day as she paraded me in front of a mirror, my scalp smarting like it was on fire. Seeing my reflection, I'd winced. Mirrors always reminded me of why I'd been brought to Fablehouse in the first place. Avoiding mirrors meant it didn't matter what colour I was, or how my hair looked; I could just get on with being me and forget about being one of them 'Brown Babies' that no one here wanted.

'HEATHER!'

I crept down the second staircase. Arlene's singing soared through the corridors. I was relieved to share a room with her, though she never stopped singing. She was a year younger than me, but nowhere near as annoying as the other ten-year-olds here, Ruth and Martha.

I could still hear Arlene as I sidled down the last staircase and eased out the back door.

Of all the orphanages I'd been in, so far Fablehouse didn't seem that bad. I'd not seen anything that made me want to run away – yet. They treated us nice, and we had plenty to eat. Miss Isolde, the headmistress, had told me that it was her life's work to make sure we'd all grow up to be 'Productive Members of Society'.

'We may seem rather unusual here, Heather,' she'd said, when the sleek silver car dropped me off, 'but you'll soon see that everything comes from the very deepest desire to ensure you flourish!'

So, every morning we had reading, writing and arithmetic, like at a regular school. And judging by how some of them carried on, it was the first time they'd done any learning. There was a Miss Clara – she was in training to be a schoolteacher, so she taught us. In the afternoons, we had free time to play as long as we stayed on the grounds. I'd explored every chance I got but hadn't discovered the best escape route yet – should I need to run. The grounds would be marvellous for hide-and-seek, but you needed friends for that; and that's the last thing I wanted. I'd lived in three other orphanages and making friends was a mistake; sometimes they'd be gone without warning, or you were. Better to be a lone ranger, less chance of heartbreak.

The place was all right, but there was no denying it: us Fablehouse lot had been hushed up and hidden away. The nearest village was called Selworthy, but I hadn't been there yet. Apparently trips were limited to church on Sundays, and thankfully I'd arrived last Monday. I overheard the nurses saying that Selworthy liked to pretend we didn't exist. All because our mums got too friendly with Black soldiers and when they went back overseas . . . well, us Brown Babies were the problem left behind. That was the reason none of us would ever forget that we weren't wanted.

After counting to ten, I crept along the red-brick wall that ran the length of the house and out to the gardens. I darted past the vegetable patch and chicken coops, shushing my fingers to my lips as the chickens squawked. No sign of Miss Gloria. And as long as I kept an eye out, I'd be able to avoid Miss Clara too.

The lawns around the house stretched as far as the eye could see, green grass and big trees in every direction. Ruth and Martha played hopscotch on the paving stones while Leon and Henry were playing Snap loudly. I headed for the run-down stone building, which the others called 'the stables'. I hadn't seen any horses. Maybe Fablehouse had them once, but clearly those days were long gone.

Reaching the corner of the stables, I rounded it and stared across the large front lawn framed by gigantic oaks. Just beyond them was a thick layer of bushes and undergrowth – I thought they might lead to the sea: my ultimate destination for today's adventure.

Halfway across the front lawn, a squeaky voice came from my left.

'Oww!'

I glanced around but couldn't see anyone.

'Up 'ere. H*elp!*'

Halfway up a tree, chubby, dirty knees flapped about, with one scruffy boot dangling off a foot. I stared upwards into tangled branches.

'What're you *doing*?' I muttered.

A mournful, mud-streaked little boy's face looked down. 'I was gettin' me ball but it's stuck an' ...' His voice rose, tears cresting a wave. 'Now I can't get down!'

It was Davey, mischievous, mop-haired and the youngest in Fablehouse; he was only six, and everyone cooed over him. I always liked younger kids in the other homes I'd been in – they told it to you straight. Life would be a lot easier if grown-ups took a leaf out of their book.

I tutted – how on earth had he got himself stuck up there? 'Lean over that big branch, give me your hand, and I'll help you.'

He wriggled to lie almost flat on the branch I pointed at and tried to stretch his fingers to meet mine, but it was no use. No way could I reach him.

After huffing and puffing a while, he started bawling. 'Lloyd!'

'L*loyd?*'

7

What did Davey want *him* for? Lloyd was probably in the common room, helping the staff, telling them how much he knew about everything. He was such a goody-goody. The sort who'd tell on you if it'd save his own skin. But I'd noticed that sometimes he forgot to put on his helpful humble-orphan act: his mouth turned down, and those big hazel eyes glazed over, dark and sorrowful, full of unspoken hurts. He was only a year older than me, but sometimes he looked like a sad old man.

'Now you listen up – Lloyd ain't here,' I snapped. Then I softened my tone, cos bless Davey – the way he trembled, clinging to that cracked branch, it wasn't going to hold out much longer.

'I can help you. If you want.' I added as an afterthought, 'I'm Heather.'

'Heffver.' Davey wiped his snotty nose with the back of his hand, and then an almighty crack sounded out as he fell, down, down – into my waiting outstretched arms.

'It's OK. I gotcha.'

I buckled under his wriggling, wailing weight and we both tumbled backwards into the grass. From

8

up high I'd thought he'd be as light as a feather, but he was a right lump; nearly crushed me.

'Oh! Thank goodness.' Miss Clara barrelled across the lawn, pinafore flying and arms outstretched, her boot laces flapping. 'Davey! *Heather!* Davey!'

I didn't want to hang around for the crushing kisses and what-have-yous, so I jumped up and pegged it through bushes and tangled weeds towards the tree-lined lanes leading away from the house.

'See youse later!' I cried over my shoulder.

'Be back for supper!' was the last thing I heard as Miss Clara focused all her attention on Davey.

Wandering off hadn't been allowed at the places I'd lived before, and I still couldn't quite believe that no one ever chased after me here. But they didn't. I asked Arlene about it on my first night. She'd snorted and said, 'Well, even if we go gadding about, we stick out like a sore thumb, don't we? Anything amiss an' the bobbies will drag you back before you can say Bob's your uncle!'

The clattering noises from Fablehouse faded the deeper into the undergrowth I went, the sweet scent of the hanging baskets lingering.

Finally I could hear myself think. Finally . . . I was away from it all. I breathed as deeply as I could, feeling my stomach lift and the breeze tickle my nostrils as I exhaled. I tramped my own path through the scratchy undergrowth and long grass.

Yesterday afternoon we'd had a 'Nature Nurture' lesson with Miss Isolde. She'd showed us how you could boil stinging nettles to make tea and wrap dock leaves around a graze. She claimed trees, flowers and plants had their own unique magic; told us how trees cared for each other, gave each other space, and said we ought to do the same. It was a bit odd, to be honest. She'd drifted off mid-sentence a few times, with a faraway look in her eyes. But now, in this place, all the interesting things she'd said came rushing back to me. She had a funny way of looking at the world and I liked it.

Although it was June, the sun was hidden now, branches thick with leaves blotting out the sky. I shuddered, rubbing my arms. I stomped past bushes and grey squirrels scampered out of my way.

I knew that Fablehouse owned loads of land. I'd only been in Miss Isolde's office once, for my welcome meeting when I'd first arrived, but I'd seen the huge, illustrated maps on the walls revealing twisty winding lanes, dense forested areas, and paths which led across moors, all the way to the sea. The other day, I'd taken a path which led to a lake, but today I wanted the sea air in my nostrils.

A wide-open plain opened up – the moorlands. Purple heather littered the heathland, which was twisted and threaded through with lime-green bracken and yellow gorse.

Now the sun was high in the sky and blazing. Walking was tough going, although my walking boots helped. A stony path sloped gently up from the moorlands and soon little hot sparks were darting up and down my calves. A sharp stabbing started in my side too, so I stopped and hoped the pain would go away. Next time I'd be better prepared and bring a drink.

But I wasn't about to turn back, so I crested the hill. In front of me was a bare-branched tree, and then a little way ahead of that, the biggest, strangest pile of rocks and stones that I'd ever seen. Miss Isolde had mentioned this little pile of stones yesterday: a cairn. The way she pronounced the word sounded like 'care-n', a Scottish word from ancient times. She'd said no one knew who had piled so many stones in one place, or why. But there must have been a reason. The stones were taller than me and formed a rough solid column. I couldn't work out how they stayed stuck together, but the cairn stood firm, like it was unbreakable. The views around were endless too. One side was open heathland, and the other was close to a cliff edge that overlooked the wild, foamy sea.

Walking closer to the gigantic pile, the oddest thing happened. The ever-present chattering in my mind, which told me I'd never be good enough, that no one would ever want me, that I was stupid – the endless marching band – fluttered to a standstill. The birds quietened. Everything hushed. 'Calm down,' people said to me when my temper flared, as it often did because there was so much to rage against. I wasn't comfortable with calm, wasn't used to feeling safe, and yet here, suddenly, a feeling of being protected shivered through my bones, almost a whisper: *We will hold you.*

As I walked closer to the cairn, my stomach swooshed, like when you cycle down a steep hill with your hands off the handlebars, feeling completely free but wild too, especially if you're yelling at the same time.

I'd reached the stones. I let my fingertips linger, touching each one to connect. Staring up at this tall column, I wondered why and who and when? It felt as if I glowed from the inside, like lights flickering inside me.

Some edges were smooth and cool, and some jagged. I felt slightly sleepy, dazed. Like a fat cat in the sun: full and contented at the same time.

The wind whisked and rustled through the gorse, and I heard a sudden rumbling noise ... from the stones? It sounded like the belly of the world groaning from underneath the earth, and my fingers snapped away, tingling warm. What had happened? Had I done something?

My stomach spiked, as if something was about to happen. The air itself was thrumming, electric, poised. Excitement edged with trepidation scurried up my outstretched arms as flashes of goosebumps followed, raised, waiting.

Then: twigs and branches cracking.

Chapter Two

The Roamers

'Who are you?' A girl's reedy voice.

I spun round, blinking the sun out of my eyes.

A stocky boy with red hair and a girl with thin yellow plaits and an even thinner face gawped at me. They were both pale-skinned, so weren't from Fablehouse. Maybe from the village? The boy was twice my size and glaring at me, but the girl? I could take her, if it came to that, even though she looked older.

'What do you mean, who am I?' I griped, annoyed at being disturbed, the peace I'd felt only moments ago now replaced by my heart slamming against my ribs. 'Who are *you*, more like?' I didn't want no trouble, but if they was gonna cause it then I'd be ready.

The lad had fat freckled cheeks and hands like slabs of beef. He stepped forward, puffing out his chest. When his eyes met mine, he narrowed his and sneered.

'You're one of *them*.'

I rolled my eyes. One of *them*? I was a few 'thems' . . . Now, which one was he talking about?

His top lip curled and the way he jutted out his chin reminded me of the Fablehouse chickens, and I nearly laughed, but I swallowed that urge because the girl's fists were bunched and her twisted expression was meaner than a mad dog's.

In other homes, sometimes the staff were handy with a belt or strap. I quickly learned that laughing or smiling – even if it was just nerves – was the worst thing to do. People do not like being laughed at.

'What are you even doing out here, *darkie*?' the boy barked.

I held my breath. I wasn't going to take his bait,

though I knew the likes of him would keep on goading.

'Yeah!' The girl smirked. She jerked her thumb towards the sea. 'Go back to where you came from.'

Back to where? Where exactly *did* I belong? I ignored the comment – I'd heard similar before – and instead clenched my fists, mirroring the girl. Another thing I'd learned was you don't run. Even when your legs are quivering, and your heart pounding, you *never* run.

Stand your ground, whispered the wind. My ground? Yes, this was my place. *Mine*. Without even thinking, I'd moved closer to the cairn. I put my hands behind me, and my palms met the stones, as if they'd give me power or protection. Soft, damp moss cooled my hot fingertips. My feet were planted firm, solid – like they were made of stone. Like the cairn; forever here. Don't run or show fear. Don't feed bullies scraps. If they knew that underneath my gritted teeth and clenched jaw I was trembling harder than rain on a leaf, then I'd be done for.

'What are *you* doing here?' I asked. 'All this land belongs to Fablehouse.'

The girl's plaits whipped in the breeze. 'This land don't belong to you.' She sounded so outraged, you'd think her own fair hands had built this whole place. 'My ma says you lot are an abomination!'

The boy spat on the ground. 'My dad says the woman who runs that broken-down old home is a . . . *freak*! A weird old witch! Dad reckons you darkies should be put to work. Do something useful for us who put food in your bellies.'

I stared at the horrible globule of spit and leaned back on the stones a little, feeling their support and weight. A sharp edge dug into my lower back, forced my mouth open.

'I ain't working for no one. Nor going anywhere neither.'

The girl's tight sneer vanished. 'Leave, or . . .'

'Or?' My throat burned with anger. I felt that if I opened my mouth any wider, I could scorch her with the fire from my heart.

'Or we'll make you,' said the boy. He rolled up his sleeves and picked up a stone. He turned it over in his palm before throwing it close enough to hit my boot.

I stared at the stone.

With that first stone thrown, silence fell over us, a wisp of menace now on the wind. Decisions needed to be made, and fast. Fight or flight?

Lightning quick, I rushed forward and bopped the girl on the nose. She staggered back, surprised, cupping her nose, eyes shiny with tears.

I'd gone and done it now; I wished the cairn could swallow me whole. I was out here alone and no one knew it. It was two against one. I prepared myself – no time for regrets. I crouched, preparing to tackle Red – take his legs out from under him, and then I'd run.

Red lumbered forward, pulling his arm back, hand in a fist ...

'Ow!' He stumbled, whipping his head around, as something glanced off his cheek.

'Bog off!' cried a voice that I recognised. Arlene?

I rolled back my shoulders and stood up straight. Arlene, Nat and Lloyd leaned out from behind the tree in the glade and raced towards us.

I hadn't spoken much to any of them really. Although me and Arlene shared a room, all I knew about her was she liked to sing day and night. She loved having her hair done; always looking perfect, her hair in fancy plaits tied with red ribbons and bows. Nat was nine and excitable as a puppy, always wanting to play, chattering away to the chickens, and practising magic tricks to anyone who'd watch and ... well, I'd already formed my theories about Lloyd.

What were they doing here? I did not need rescuing.

The girl screamed, 'No one wants you!'

'Says who?' Nat shrieked back, fierce. His usual goofy grin wiped out.

'*My ma* says you lot should get lost!'

Striding forward, hands on hips, Arlene said, 'Bet your ma wishes she could get rid of *you* an' all!'

'You tryin' be smart?' the boy grunted, frowning.

Arlene poked her tongue out. 'I don't really need to *try* ...'

Red looked like he wanted to thrash her. Although the village kids were bigger and older, they exchanged a shifty glance like they must have known, sensed somehow, that they weren't a match for the four of us.

'Animals!' the boy muttered, scuffing up dirt as he backed off.

'ROAR!' hollered Nat, hooking his fingers into claws and baring his gnashers. I stifled a laugh.

'Let's go – c'mon, Mary.'

'Bye, Scary Mary!' Arlene chirruped, giving her the V.

I'd settled back, leaning into the cairn, just watching them. Lloyd was too. I felt protected and supported, but not because the three of them were here. It was something else.

Mary sneered. 'When we get back to the village, we're gonna tell on you.'

Arlene howled with laughter. 'Tell who what?'

'We're gonna let everyone know that you lot are wild! You'll get in trouble and then they'll close down that rotten home for good. You'll be in the gutter. It'll serve you right!'

'Don't you mess with us Fablehouse kids!' Lloyd shouted at their retreating figures. 'Or *you'll* be sorry!'

The village kids scrambled down the rocky path and across the heathland until they'd vanished.

'I coulda had them,' I grumbled, uncomfortable at the way Nat, Arlene and Lloyd were now grinning at me, as if we were a team or something.

Smiling, Lloyd said, 'What's wrong with having a little help, Heather?'

I bit down hard on my lip, ridding myself of the irritation and racing feelings, leaving behind only a familiar fog of not being able to say what I was really feeling. I realised that Lloyd hadn't apologised or tried to make friends with those kids. I thought he'd be the turncoat type, avoiding trouble at any opportunity, but he'd . . . stood up for me. They all had, and they didn't even know me.

Nat shoved his hands into his pockets and booted a pebble. 'Why's it have to always be like that – us and them?'

'Dunno.' Lloyd shrugged. 'It's not right, is it?' And once again, that quietness I sometimes glimpsed behind his eyes – an expression I recognised – vanished as quickly as it had appeared, and he was sunny optimism again. 'Anyway, we got rid of them well and good!'

Threat gone, I peered at the three of them, frowning. 'Whatcha doing out here anyway?'

They all avoided my gaze. Nat started picking his nose and Arlene smoothed down her pinafore with one hand and her hair with the other.

'Did you . . . *follow* me?' I asked, surprised.

Arlene's expression was haughty. 'No, we did not!'

Lloyd scratched his head, his short black curls bouncing. 'We were going to ask if *you* followed *us*, actually.' He rearranged the satchel strap around his shoulder, fingers touching the buckle.

I squinted suspiciously. 'What?'

'Well . . .' Nat bounced up and down, full of energy, like he was on springs. 'This is *our* place. This spot, right here.' He spread out his arms, wide. 'The Stony Tower, the view of the sea.'

I huffed. 'It has a proper name. Miss Isolde said so. It's a cairn.'

Nat pouted. 'Don't care. I call it the Stony Tower cos that's what it is. We always come here together.' He glanced at Arlene for confirmation. 'Lloyd leads the way, he knows the best shortcuts.'

'Without him we always get lost.' Arlene nodded, arms folded. 'Yep. We tell stories and make stuff up.'

'And it's funny –' Lloyd thrust his hands in his pockets – 'because whichever path I take from Fablehouse, we always wind up here somehow. This place is . . . perfect. Special. We all feel it. I mean, know it.'

He turned his head away, towards the sea, the sun glittering on the water. 'It's a place to come and just ... be ourselves. I feel peaceful here. Happy. Makes me feel close to people I don't see no more.' His voice dipped. 'Probably sounds silly to you.'

He turned to me, but I couldn't look at him and dropped my gaze. My heart wanted to say It *doesn't sound silly at all*, but the words wouldn't form; they were blocked, trapped right there in my throat. It was often like that, I couldn't speak cos the words always came out wrong.

But even if I understood, I still didn't want the cairn to be their place! This was mine – I needed it. I didn't have anywhere else. My throat burned, which meant hot tears weren't far away. I gulped them down. Last thing I wanted to do here, in front of this lot, was to start bawling like a baby. But since Mum being taken away, this was the first place where I'd felt good. I didn't want to give it up; I'd only just found it.

'Why don't you never play with us, Heather?' Nat whined.

Lloyd threw him a warning look, but Nat was right: I'd kept myself to myself since arriving. Even with twelve other kids around, it was easy to keep your distance. The adults didn't bother us as long as we stayed neat, respectful and did our chores.

'You never asked me,' I said sharply. Prickles of shame itched my neck; I knew I could have made more effort.

Arlene snorted. 'You don't get given an invite,' she said, 'you just join in. Everyone's welcome.' She started singing and dancing around the cairn.

'What's that song?' I asked, twirling round to watch her.

'One of Dickie Valentine's.'

'Valentine? Sounds like a love song.'

'They were Mummy's favourites.' Arlene spun around with her arms outstretched. 'She says all songs are about love when you really think about it.'

'Look. We can share this place.' Lloyd was suddenly next to me, leaning against the cairn, smiling. Not one of his flashy grins neither, but a genuine shy smile. He started touching the stones. When his fingers bumped into mine, I gasped – unaware that I had been moving my fingers too, doing the same, feeling the stones' jagged edges.

'How do you think they got to be, like ... stuck together?' I asked, snapping my fingers away. 'Why don't they just topple over?'

'Not sure.' Lloyd's hazel eyes, close to tiger-stripes, sparkled. 'Some sort of glue or cement, maybe?'

Nat had his hands up under his chin, wrinkling his nose, making snuffling noises. 'More like magic!' He sniffed.

Arlene said, 'Think the pile was built *for* something?'

'Or some*one* maybe?' Nat's eyes suddenly widened, and he pointed across the heathland. 'Ooh, a real rabbit!' and then he sprinted down the rocky paths. 'Let's follow where it goes!' he shouted.

Arlene whooped and grabbed my hand, pulling me across the moorland. She swung our arms in the air together and it was so unexpected to be tangled up in someone else's joy that I just let her.

Lloyd caught up to Nat, who'd collapsed on to the grass at the end of the moorland. 'It got away!' he moaned, out of breath. 'Aww, I wanted to train it to pop out of a hat after I do my tricks.'

Arlene sat on the grass and, still holding my hand,

pulled me down too. She eased off her boots and lay back. We could glimpse the top of the cairn, and part of me felt like I was back there with it, still leaning against those stones and feeling their sun-baked warmth.

'Here.' Lloyd brought out a glass bottle from his satchel and passed it to a breathless Nat.

'So, Heather,' Nat said, after taking a huge gulp. 'What would you do if you found half a crown?'

'Oh, I don't know. Get on a bus and go somewhere, I s'pose. What would you do?'

Nat grinned, before laughing and saying, 'Look for the other half!'

He passed the bottle to Arlene, and then, when it reached me, I guzzled the sweet-sour liquid: lemonade. The cool sharpness refreshed me. I hadn't realised how thirsty I was, how much I needed this.

'That's good, thanks.' I stood up and handed the bottle to Lloyd. 'Where did you get it?'

Lloyd took a drink himself. 'Sometimes Miss Gloria will make us up a picnic. She said I'm to make sure Nat and Arlene don't get lost, hurt or ... too parched. We're to come back in one piece for supper.'

Arlene said, 'Lloyd's the oldest, he's twelve, so he gets to be in charge.'

'No one's in charge of me.' I flashed Lloyd a warning glance; if he even so much as tried to boss me about, he'd soon think better of it.

'I just know my way round here, that's all,' he said, as if reading my mind. 'But I'm not the boss.'

'We's equal,' Nat said, nodding at each of us. 'And we stick together.'

Arlene moved over to me and linked my arm with hers. 'I always wanted a sister. We can be each other's family, right?'

Why were they so bloomin' pally? They'd only spoken to me five minutes ago.

'I've got a family,' I said stubbornly, pulling my arm out of Arlene's tight grip and inching away, not bothered if she noticed or not. 'Don't need another one, ta.'

'We all have,' Lloyd said. 'But the point is, they're not here with us now, are they?'

'Lloyd says we're "all in the same boat",' Nat added.

Sitting back down, I plucked at the daisies next to me and remembered a word I'd read once. 'Well. Mine are ... *indisposed* right now. But one day they'll come back.'

I wasn't going to tell them how my mother got so sad and sick in her mind that she couldn't get out of bed ... and then got carted off to one of them sanatoriums. My aunt and grandparents looked after me for a while but complained I got too big and too noisy and so they sent me away too.

'What about you anyway?' I retorted, turning the tables before I spilt my whole guts to this golden boy – although I wasn't so sure any more that he was quite the phoney I'd first thought he was.

Lloyd fiddled with the buckle of his satchel. 'I lived with my grampy for a while.' He didn't look at any of us.

Arlene started twirling with her arms spread out, staring up at the sky. 'Look at those clouds!' She spun round and round.

'He never talks about his mum,' Nat whispered, nudging me as if Lloyd couldn't hear us. 'He's the only one from around here, and some people were real mean about her. His gramps ain't around no more – *though he ain't dead neither, not yet.*'

Little Nat's face was as open as the heathlands, and his good nature impossible to resist.

I smiled at him. 'And what about you then?'

'Me?' Nat wriggled a stubby finger up his nose. 'Oh, I always been 'ere; came when I was two. I may as well be borned in the kitchen, so Miss Gloria says!' He rolled on to his stomach, flicking a strand of grass, trying to knock off a ladybird crawling up it. 'I don't remember anything else.'

'I'm dizzy!' Arlene had stopped spinning, and now staggered around dramatically. I shifted over in case she was going to topple on to me.

Arlene flopped down, arms spread. 'My mother went to America to marry my father – looks just like Nat King Cole, he does. He's a pilot, but she couldn't take me with her because the plane was *very* small. She's an actress.' Arlene's brown eyes shone, but her voice cracked a little. 'She has to get to Hollywood first, but they'll come back.'

Was that true? The way her eyes lit up told me that she really believed what she was saying, but I'd spent years waiting for visits to happen – the letter or phone call to arrive – and they never did. I knew by now not to expect diddly-squat.

Grown-ups told lies to keep us quiet, and to stop us asking questions, but they never understood that lies just made sure we did neither.

I fell silent, rolling over on to my tummy, and gazed back towards the cairn. Something like cornstalks rustling, or insects murmuring underneath the earth, stirred and shifted as the world soaked up our half-truths and wishes – all the tall tales we'd told since we were old enough to speak. None of us mentioned the thoughts that woke us in the middle of the night: what if no one ever came for us? What if we *were* alone, forever? What then?

I shivered, cold flashing over me suddenly, like icicles being shoved down my pinafore.

'We should get back, or Miss Gloria'll be out for blood.'

I stood up and brushed myself down.

'We *have* been gone for ages,' Lloyd agreed, packing his bottle away.

We walked back across the moorlands, then through the long fields, the fat bees buzzing. Nat chattered to Lloyd, who listened and laughed but didn't say much, and Arlene sang. The song rhymed 'blue' and 'do'. I had the urge to add in '*shooby-dooby-do*' but I didn't. After a while, I fell into step next to her.

Her voice was soft and slow, and every now and then I glanced over my shoulder, checking that the cairn was still there as we moved fifty, and then a hundred, and then two hundred yards away from it. Checking that it would wait for me.

Arlene's voice got louder, and warmed me through any time I slipped into shadow. She had a really good voice. When she reached certain high notes, it made my insides wobble.

As we approached Fablehouse, the sun had cooled in the sky. We'd been gone two, maybe three hours. My stomach rumbled, reminding me I was starving.

Miss Gloria and another nursery nurse, Miss Betty, stood on the doorstep, arms folded. Judy and Jeremiah, the nine-year-old twins who I'd never once heard speak, poked their heads out from behind the nurses' aprons.

'We were ready to send out a search party for youse,' Miss Gloria admonished.

'We lost track of time, miss. We're very sorry,' Lloyd said, his big brown eyes the picture of sincerity.

'Shall we lay the table?' he asked.

I rolled my eyes seeing how Miss Betty practically melted at his feet.

He always took the grown-ups' side, but I guessed that made it easier to keep the peace. If he never gave no trouble, then they wouldn't be looking for any. Clever of him to be so well behaved, now that I came to think of it. Maybe there was more to him than met the eye.

'Well, hurry – go along now and clean up for supper!' Miss Betty said, waving us all inside.

'Heather!' Miss Gloria's smiling eyes landed on me. 'Look at the state of you.' She reached into the front of her apron, bringing out her famous comb. The metal spikes gleamed, catching the last of the afternoon sunlight.

'I may be a state,' I retorted, 'but that don't mean I'm ready for one of your brushings . . .'

She laughed. 'You can't escape me and my comb forever!'

'I'll keep trying!'

The nursery nurses stepped aside and the four of us headed through the double doors and into the big entrance hall. The grandfather clock clanged loudly.

'Wash behind your ears too – smart as you like, please!' Miss Betty called after us. 'Right lot of little roamers, you are.' She chuckled.

'Less of the little!' Lloyd replied cheekily.

He winked at me, and I suddenly saw straight through to the real him; it was like a punch in the guts. There wasn't any fakery; he just thought he needed to try really hard, all the time. He believed that being a good boy was the key – to happiness, to understanding, to the world opening up for him.

'Just roamers will do nicely,' I added, grinning back.

The Roamers. I liked that.

Chapter Three

Dead Arthur

There was no escaping Miss Gloria's brush-and-comb combination a few days later because I'd been summoned to Miss Isolde's office. As I walked down the long, quiet corridor, I couldn't help but nibble my fingernails.

The door was open. Miss Isolde was bent over boxes of books spread out in the middle of the carpet. She looked up.

'Heather!' She beckoned me inside. 'Good, good. Come on in.'

Stepping through the heavy, wooden door, I rested my hand on the shiny brass doorknob, uncertain if I should shut it.

'You can leave it open, dear.'

I stood with my hands held loosely behind my back, as I was told was polite.

'Miss Gloria and Miss Betty inform me that you've formed quite a ... tight-knit group with Lloyd, Nat and Arlene over the last couple of days?'

Kneeling and rifling through another box, she pushed aside a strand of black hair that had escaped out of a neat bun. She stacked books into piles before sitting back on her heels and smiling.

What was she expecting me to say? I didn't know what she wanted from me, but she must have wanted something. Adults always did. I shrugged, then corrected myself and shook out my shoulders, remembering that shrugging was considered rude, ignorant. She probably needed to know I wasn't going to be any trouble, for her or for Fablehouse. Maybe she'd been warned about me running away, heard about my tantrums and thought I was a bad influence. But I liked the others, and I liked how they liked me, and I didn't want her stopping that.

'Yes, we've been playing at the cairn ...' I drifted off to look around her office. A large wooden desk was covered in leather-bound books, scattered papers and a typewriter. Behind the desk, lattice windows looked out on to the front lawn. She should move her office around; you'd want to be looking out on to trees and flowers, not some dusty old pictures on the walls.

'You've become inseparable, so they tell me. I'm delighted to hear that.'

Oh. *Good*. I relaxed slightly.

'They're very special children; I believe you'll be good for one another. Lloyd is an excellent chess player, very sensible head on those young shoulders, I must say. And the cairn is exquisite, isn't it? Just be mindful of those cliff tops.'

I nodded, thinking of how happy that place made me. Every day that week, as soon as lunch was over, we'd be out for hours until we had to head back for supper. We alternated between playing cops and robbers, princes and princesses, cowboys and Indians ... there were no limits. The weather was always perfect, and we never disagreed.

Wherever I'd been before, I always felt that I was

never quite right somehow. I was too much of this or not enough of that. So gradually I'd always ended up on the outside – never really part of any particular group. And over the years, I'd told myself that I didn't care about being left out, that it was better to just rely on myself, but the Roamers were different. They took me as I was. No one raised an eyebrow when I laughed too loudly or got overexcited, none of them told me I should be anything else. They listened to me, asked me what I thought and waited for my answer, and they never wanted nothing. I never imagined I'd ever find such good friends. We were the same, but not the same.

Miss Isolde stood and leaned against her desk, smoothing down her navy-blue dress. Her face was thin and pale, with high cheekbones, always dotted pink. Her eyes were set wide apart, and she had a tiny birthmark, almost in the shape of an anchor, just under her chin.

'When you first arrived, you kept yourself rather ... isolated and, I admit, I was worried. I didn't want to crowd you and so I kept my distance, but now it seems you may really be settling in?'

She laced her long fingers together. A beautiful purple ring was on her right hand – no wedding ring. Unlike the other homes I'd been in, she was the first headmistress I'd known without grey or white hair.

'Yes. It feels like . . .' But I couldn't find the words, and my tongue stuck to the roof of my mouth.

'Home?' she said hopefully. Her eyes were very blue, tinged with lilac, like bluebells.

Home? Wasn't sure I'd go that far. 'I like it here. It's . . . There's lots of space.'

'Good.' She looked pleased. 'I do hope you find this an environment that you don't want to run away from.'

What could I say to that?

'Yes, ma'am. I mean, no. No.'

'A feeling of space, of freedom, is exactly what I like for all my children.' She coughed, and quickly corrected herself. 'For the children who live here, who pass through our doors. It's important Fablehouse isn't seen as simply another orphanage. I like to trust everyone – until they prove otherwise. Do you understand what I mean by trust, Heather?'

Trust. I nodded. That meant she'd leave me alone until I messed up.

'Trust is the bedrock. The only way forward is with grace and kindness, and every child under this roof should understand those are Fablehouse's values. That everyone is accepted for who they are.'

I rolled my feet in and out, waiting. This sounded very nice and all, but when was the BUT coming? There always was one.

She cleared her throat. 'The thing is . . . there's no nice way to say this, but I'm afraid a complaint has been lodged with the local council.'

'A complaint?' I swallowed.

'Apparently an innocent child was struck on the nose.' She stared at me pointedly, but I pressed my lips together tight.

Those village kids!

'By – and I quote – a "hellion with wild curls" . . .' She traced her fingertips along the spine of a big book on the desk in front of her.

'A whatta?'

'A hellion.'

Then I did shrug. 'An' what's that when it's at home?'

She almost looked through me. 'A demon.'

'Oh.' I looked everywhere but into her eyes. I dragged my boot along the thick, dark carpet. *Was I in trouble? What would happen now?* I looked at the paintings on the wall, of the local landscapes, a map of the grounds, and wondered why she had so many different images of the cairn. *Oh please ... don't forbid me from going there!*

Her eyes stayed steady on me, and the silence grew, filling up like a drain about to overflow. I did not want to be here when the gunk came flooding out.

'It weren't me that started it!' I finally burst out. 'I was minding my own business!' The injustice of being called here for a scolding, and probably being sent away, made my voice come out too loud. 'They – they called you a witch!'

'Heather!' Miss Isolde held up her palm, and I fell silent and stared at the carpet; traced the patterns. When I looked up again, she didn't seem cross. No switch had been brought out from under her desk; I heard no clang of a strap or belt buckle.

'I'm on your side, Heather, *if* there were sides to be had. It's my job, my ... mission to protect the children in my care, and that's exactly what I intend to do. I will deal with this. Those children had no right to even be on our land; we may need to take steps to prevent trespassers in future. But the further from the house you explore, the more careful you'll need to be. This is your home, but you can't simply go around thumping people whom you don't like!'

She strode across the room to straighten a watercolour of the land around the cairn. The cairn was off to one side, and the sea raged below it. The contrast between the foaming, white-tipped waves and the grey stones, edged with what looked like silver flames, reminded me of how I often felt inside.

'Fablehouse is ... well, there is less funding than before. Caretakers can no longer attend to the gardens and grounds. We need the council and local people on our side. We need to pitch in and help each other; responsibility falls to us in many respects. Fablehouse will be assessed and carefully watched by the authorities now, I'm sure – so it's vital that you understand about ... consequences.'

Uh-oh. Here it was. What would my punishment be?

'Since you appear to like rising early – you can assist Cook with the breakfasts this week. Making porridge and cream for thirteen is no mean feat. After lunch you will gather the vegetables for supper.'

Miss Isolde ran her fingertips along the top of the gilt-edged frame. 'Apparently the altercation happened at the cairn.'

A statement, not a question.

'Yes, miss.'

I expected an explanation of how dangerous, or off limits, the cairn was – not a place for children – but she gave a long, quiet sigh. It could have been a trick of the sunlight streaming through the windows, but her eyes almost looked wistful. She went and sat back behind her desk.

'The cairn. It's marvellous, isn't it? I like to walk there of an evening sometimes. Often the most extraordinary insights come to me at dusk.'

I thought of those rocks, the sea, and the moorland all around – the air charged with wildness and freedom; how peace settled over me like a shield the moment my fingers reached for those stones. How each day, it was as if the stones gave me more nourishment. How I always came away feeling stronger and my mind clearer, my breath easier. My dreams were gentle and pleasant, and I never woke myself up crying in the night any more. I knew us Roamers all felt the same. I could see it.

Day after day, Lloyd and I almost finished each other's sentences when we were at the cairn. We could never beat each other playing rock, paper, scissors because we always chose the same option. Whatever song Arlene sang seemed to fit my exact mood. Nat noticed something new every time, pointed out sights we'd have missed otherwise: the sheen on a snail's shell or the unfurling of a fern, and his magic tricks never went wrong! Even when I couldn't find the right words, they still understood what I was trying to say – it was in the way they looked at me and really saw me. *Me*. And for me it was the same. Often words didn't even fit; I'd just sense what the Roamers needed, or how they were feeling.

'We go there every day.'

Miss Isolde gazed at me for longer than I felt comfortable having someone stare. Her face softened and, for a second, she looked as young as Miss Gloria.

'It is quite far,' she said, fingers steepled under her chin.

It was about a mile to the cairn, and even Nat, cheerful as he was, whined most of the way.

'Can you ride a bicycle?'

'I have done before,' I replied. 'They had one at my last place.'

'Well. If you aren't afraid of a little elbow grease, then there are three old and very rusty bicycles in the shed. Maybe you could fix them up? Teach the others how to ride if they don't know how?'

Oh! If we had bicycles, we could explore the land even more. The Stony Tower, as Nat called it, was my favourite place, but there was so much more to discover. This land felt full of secrets just waiting to be unearthed. Some days the sea called to me, and I hadn't been back to the lake yet. Sometimes the earthy forests drew my attention ... I'd gaze up at the trees and their lush green leaves waving as we passed under them on our way to the cairn.

'Yes, miss!'

'Before you leave, come and help me with these, please.' She indicated a large cardboard box by the door, also filled with books.

We pushed and wiggled the box across the carpet until it was under her desk. I grunted and wiped my forehead. 'What are these for?'

'I'm extending the Fablehouse library!' Her face glowed with pride. 'We received donations from the parish, and I found boxes in the attic too. Even though I grew up here, I never had any notion the attic hid such treasures.'

'Is this your family's house?' I asked, surprised.

'I thought of them as my family, yes. I was adopted when I was five. My mother died in childbirth, after having my sisters – twins – and my grandmother disappeared.' Her smile was a little sad. 'See? Everyone has their stories, Heather. Everyone has someone lost to them, one way or another.'

She moved over to the big armchair by the window and stared across the lawn. 'Remember that storm the other night? I kept dreaming of my grandmother's herb garden and her cottage. I dreamed of books falling through the ceiling, with strange symbols dancing off their pages ... The next thing I knew, I was checking the attic for leaks, and that's when I found the box.'

She swept the papers on her desk to one side, dragging an enormous brown leather book forward. 'Isn't this one magnificent? It even has a lock.'

The book was four or five times the size of any book I'd seen. The cover was worn, scratches and marks criss-crossing its leather. The lock had a gold panel with a keyhole, and thin gold chains connecting the hinges.

I'd never seen a book with a lock before and my heart pounded with excitement about what might be hidden inside.

'Do you have a key?'

'I haven't found one, but I've more unpacking to do,' she said. 'I *will* find the key. I'm not having knowledge locked away!'

I stared at the squiggles and strange shapes made of triangles and circles scratched into the cover. 'What are those symbols and signs?'

'I'm not sure, but they're very mysterious, aren't they?'

'Hmm.' I nodded and traced my fingers over the markings. A fluttering pulsed in my stomach, similar to how I'd felt when I was near the cairn, but I paused.

My fingertips stiffened as a flicker of something shadowy passed through my mind. I snatched my fingers away. It was like seeing a maggot wriggle out of an apple, or lifting a rock and finding woodlice and beetles squirming beneath. I rubbed my fingers quickly up and down my pinafore.

'And what's *that* book about?' I pointed to another on her desk. Two men in shiny silver armour were on horseback. Lush hills and colourful flags were in the background. Miss Isolde pushed it closer to me, so I could read the title: *Le Morte d'Arthur*.

'Is that French?' I wasn't a great reader, but I did like the sounds of words, rolling them around on my tongue, and in my mind.

'The title is French. It means *The Death of Arthur*, but the stories inside are written in English. Have you heard the legend of King Arthur? The stories are about a very old English king from a long time ago, knights on quests, rescuing maidens, all that type of fun. Apparently it was my grandmother's. And funnily enough, I'm named after one of the characters. Borrow it for as long as you like, and I'll see you at lunch.'

I picked up the large book and, beaming, cradled it to my chest. A book of my very own! Before she got sick, Mum had read *The Wizard of Oz* and *Alice in Wonderland* to me, and I spent hours imagining having adventures and discovering magical lands of my own.

As I walked slowly down the corridor and up the stairs to my room, I wondered what I'd discover between these pages. The cover looked thrilling! Life so far hadn't really been the kind of exciting adventure I'd hoped for. I couldn't wait to find out who this Dead Arthur was.

Chapter Four

The Meeting

The next day, after breakfast duty, cleaning out the chicken coops and collecting vegetables, me and Lloyd were in the shed, on our hands and knees, with a toolbox, a bucket of water and oily wire scrubbers. It was a good place to be because there had been a wild summer storm in the night and the rain hadn't stopped all morning.

We were ready to get to work. We'd sent Nat and Arlene off to play. They'd tried to help, but Arlene did more singing than scrubbing and twirled so much that she knocked over the bucket, while Nat, trying to spin a spanner, nearly had my eye out. Lloyd and

I decided we'd be better off doing the bikes up ourselves.

I rolled up my sleeves, ready to get started, though I kept glancing at the Dead Arthur book that I'd brought along in my lap. I couldn't stop staring at the pictures of kings and gold crowns and graceful long-haired women in elegant blue robes. Why didn't my hair ever look like these pictures – long and smooth and silky? My hair wouldn't have laid flat no matter what was done to it. I had a flash of my mother, ironing her long thick hair, how it always flowed over her shoulders. I used to wrap it round my face sometimes, like a comforting blanket.

'I used to deliver newspapers by bicycle when I lived with Grampy,' Lloyd said. 'There was nothin' he didn't know about fixing up bikes. First thing we do is get rid of as much rust as we can,' he added, passing me wire wool which stank to high heaven. 'It's oiled up. Now just grab a hold of the frame, and go round in little circles, trying to get the rust off. Watch out, cos it'll be as slippery as juggling eels.'

The strong smell clogged up my throat, but after a while I got used to it. Lloyd and I quietly scrubbed the rust off the three bikes, going up and down the spokes, but it was a comfortable silence and made a change from Nat's jokes and Arlene's singing. Being here, with my new friend, made me feel warm and quiet inside, like sipping hot milk.

I stole a sideways glance at him. Did he feel it too? This warmth that kept all the bad feelings away? I felt it even more strongly when we were at the cairn, when we were out roaming; when we'd call out to the Stony Tower, and the moors and the forests, hooting and hollering as we imagined being answered back. I'd never had this before; friends like these. It had been less than two weeks and yet I had the feeling that we'd always known each other, and that we always would. I couldn't imagine them not in my life.

After most of the rust had been dissolved, the inner tubes changed and checked, and the bikes polished with rags, I asked Lloyd, 'Does your grampy ever visit here?'

'Nope.' Lloyd sighed. 'He kept forgetting stuff. Wandering off, getting lost. One day, he fell over, and couldn't remember where he lived. That's when I got brought here. They said he couldn't look after me any more. He's in a home now.'

Poor Lloyd – no wonder he sometimes looked so sad.

'And you can't go to see him?'

'It's not near here.' Lloyd focused on polishing the handlebars, now that he'd turned his bicycle upright again. 'And I'm not sure he'd remember who I was.'

'Ahh, who could forget you?' I said lightly.

He smiled, but a hush settled over us like a fine drizzle. I kept sneaking glances at him, polishing determinedly, but he bit down on his lip, and I knew what that meant.

'Here, try this one,' I said, passing him a clean rag. 'You're doing a good job there – be able to see your face in it soon.'

'Some might not reckon that's the best result.'

'I've seen worse faces,' I said, smiling.

His face suddenly lit up, banishing the clouds that had appeared behind his eyes. 'And I got the Roamers now, haven't I?'

He did indeed. We all did.

* * *

The rain had dried up and the sun was cooling by the time we set off for our visit to the cairn; Lloyd had to spend some time reminding Arlene how to ride because she hadn't been on a bike for ages.

'Watch out!' he called, as she wobbled off up ahead along the paths.

'What about me?' Nat grumped. 'I can't reach those pedals!'

'You can fit in there.' Lloyd pointed and Nat threw himself into the big wicker basket attached to the front of the biggest bicycle. 'And hold on to this, will ya?' Lloyd handed him a big bottle of lemonade.

Lloyd huffed and puffed, pedalling hard. Nat was skinny and small for his age, but I could tell from the way Lloyd's bike swerved all over the place that Nat was also a wriggler.

'Which way do we go now then?' I called from up front, over my shoulder.

'You're going the wrong way. Follow me and I'll lead. Nat! Stop jigging about!' Lloyd's voice carried on the wind as they overtook us and disappeared round a corner.

Arlene pulled up alongside me, stopped and touched the rusty bell on my handlebars. 'Think we can get this working?'

'Maybe,' I said. 'We'll see.'

She grinned. 'Bet it sounds wonderful!'

'Come on, keep moving!'

I cycled faster across the heathland, my heart pounding because I couldn't see Lloyd anywhere now – although I believed I could sense they'd gone *this* way – then, as I crested the little hill, the land opened up, and we glimpsed the cairn in the distance. I heard a mighty shout and saw Nat and Lloyd lying on the ground, the bike wheels spinning madly as Nat scrabbled away from the cliff edge.

Breathless, I cycled towards them and skidded to a sudden stop, followed by Arlene, just in time to see Lloyd grab Nat's arm and yank him nearer the cairn to make sure he was safe.

'Sorry! I ... I won't mess around no more!' Nat rolled away from Lloyd's grip, panting.

Arlene and I climbed off our bikes and laid them down just before the cairn.

I walked over to Lloyd, who was bent over his

bike, trying to straighten out the wheel. The bottle of lemonade was completely smashed. I kicked the glass away.

'Is your bike all right?'

'Think so,' he muttered. 'Might need to straighten out a couple of spokes. Dunno what happened.'

'Heather …' Nat's voice was shaky, and as I turned, both he and Arlene stared wide-eyed, backing away from something at the bottom of the cairn.

'That a dead body?' Arlene called out nervously, pointing a wavering finger at a lifeless shape.

I looked over at Lloyd, who grabbed a rock, readying to throw it if needed. Quick thinking.

Nat lifted his fists in front of his face but crouched behind Arlene. 'Think it's a wild animal?'

The bundle, a curled-up heap, groaned and shifted. We all stepped back.

'Ha! That's no badger!' Arlene breathed.

As the shape unfolded – legs and arms appearing – we realised it was a man. He stood up. Gasping, we stared up at him. He was very tall. My legs quivered, thighs made of ball bearings, and the moisture in my mouth vanished. *Who was he, and what was he doing here?*

'Should we r-r-run?' I stammered, not convinced my legs would get me to the tree in the glade without collapsing.

'There's four of us an' only one of him!' Lloyd whispered, not taking his eyes off the man, who was moving very slowly, straining his neck and shoulders.

As well as being very tall, the man was broad, and dark-skinned, with a wide-open face. His skin was darker than any of us at Fablehouse and glistening shiny. I didn't know about the others, but I'd never seen a dark-skinned man in real life before. Only on Lloyd's baseball cigarette cards, Jackie Robinson and the like. His clothes were unusual – a loose linen smock, and trousers of a heavy dark cloth with a leather harness, covered in bracken and stained deep green with moss.

'An' I think he's hurt – look!'

Lloyd was right, the man looked like he'd had seven bells bashed out of him by someone, his hands and arms scratched and bleeding. Still, I'd never seen anyone who looked more regal, the way he held himself, spine like a rod, chin jutting out. The hollows of his cheekbones glowed. His hair was like dark thick ropes which twisted down to his shoulders. A dimple dipped in his chin.

'Help me . . .' he croaked.

His dark eyes looked wary and he stared at us in turn. Eventually his panting slowed, as he stumbled against the cairn.

'Who are you?' Lloyd asked cautiously. He stepped in front of Nat and Arlene with his arm out as a barrier. *Protecting us.* 'This is our land.'

'Where am I?' The man put his hand to his ribs and bent over, wincing. 'I . . . I . . .'

He was in pain. Helping him was all that mattered.

'Who did this to you?' I asked gently, stepping forward, fear forgotten. 'What are you doing alone out here?'

'He ain't the full shilling, it seems to me,' Arlene whispered nervously.

Perhaps I should have been more afraid, but I wasn't. He was wounded, like an animal caught in a trap, and he just needed to be freed.

Nat ducked his head under Arlene's arm and touched the man's billowing sleeve. 'Mister? What's yer name?'

'My name?' The man's voice rumbled low and rusty, as if he hadn't spoken for years. His eyes clouded, and he nodded his head, like he was about to bow. 'I – I am Pal.' His accent was strange, thick and heavy.

'Pal?' Lloyd stretched out his arm and, holding Pal's elbow, all four of us stepped forward together and eased him down into a sitting position. 'As in *friend*?'

Pal rubbed the back of his head and grimaced, his eyes fluttering closed. 'Where am I?'

'You musta come from Selworthy way,' Arlene reasoned.

'Was you ... Did you get beat up?' Lloyd asked. 'Is that what happened? Them lot from the village?'

We had the same thoughts – if those village kids weren't used to brown faces, then the likes of their parents probably hadn't seen many black-faced grown-ups neither. Nor had we, but at least we recognised our own. We would never be afraid of Pal for no reason. Why would we? He was one of us.

'I think he's *really* hurt,' I murmured to Lloyd, pointing to a tear in Pal's trousers where blood dripped from a gash on his calf.

The wind picked up, whipping around the cairn with a whistling noise. Pal turned his head slowly, studying the landscape, taking it all in.

'Methinks –' he spread his arms wide – 'I know this land, and yet the unfamiliar surrounds me.'

'We can walk with you if you're lost,' I said. 'The village is only a mile or so across the moorland. Look, out there – north? That's the Bristol Channel. And south – well, that's the Exmoor hills.'

Pal shook his head and tried to stand, but the effort made him stagger, and he sank to his knees. He moaned again – a terrible deep chilling noise – sounding like he was more than just physically hurt. Nat sensed it too and his forehead creased with worry.

'Mister!' Nat rushed forward and threw his skinny arms round Pal's neck, clinging, trying to lift him up. 'Come on, mister! You'll be all right.'

Arlene hung back a little, biting her nails. She wasn't looking at Pal.

I turned to her. 'I reckon he's more afraid of us than we need to be of him.'

She shrugged. 'Who knows? Maybe he's lost his

memory? Or ... like that criminal on the moors in that story, that *Great Expecta*—'

Lloyd pounded his hand into his fist. 'I bet it *was* them villagers. Look at how big and strong he looks! They were probably scared half to death.'

'I shall not let them through ...' Pal reached out for the cairn, his huge hands shaking, his knuckles bloody, as he grasped the stones.

I glanced at Lloyd, who was gawping at Pal with an almost pained expression. And then I remembered what he'd said earlier, about his grampy losing his memory and being confused.

Before I could open my mouth, Lloyd said the words I was thinking. 'Mr Pal, we'll help you.'

A crow sailed across the sky. I gazed up at the glossy black wings, watched a feather spiral down through the air, carried out to sea by the breeze.

'You have some cuts and scrapes there,' I said gently. 'If you come with us, we can clean you up.'

Arlene nudged me sharply, looking confused. 'What are you playing at?' she hissed.

'I dunno. He needs help, doesn't he?'

'You off your rocker?' Arlene exclaimed.

'Although ... I s'pose ... maybe Miss Isolde could call a doctor?'

'No. No grown-ups,' I said. 'They won't understand, they'll call the bobbies.'

'Well, what will we do—'

'I won't let them through ...' Pal muttered. 'Be without fear, no one shall pass ...'

His words sounded like crazy talk.

Lloyd gulped and swallowed, staring at the ground. 'Maybe it's not just his memory, maybe his mind's gone ...'

I shuddered. *Please, no.* I knew what that was like. My mother, her glassy stare, mumbling, the confusing things she said before being dragged away ...

Lloyd and I exchanged a look. Here, at the cairn, we almost had one mind, thought the same thoughts, and with that look, my mind was made up. Everyone deserved a chance. Everyone deserved to be treated with kindness and dignity. If we couldn't make sure that happened for our mothers and fathers and grandparents, then at the very least we could help this man. The longer we looked at Pal, and really saw him, the more obvious it became that there wasn't anything to be frightened of here. Not from him.

Pal wasn't mad ... he was ours. Maybe the cairn had sent him to us; we knew the cairn was special. Maybe this was our adventure – to help him.

Lloyd settled as I stared at him, and my flapping thoughts settled down too.

'You saw how them kids started on me the other day, and I hadn't done nothing. He's ... one of us.' I smiled reassuringly. I remembered passages from the book I'd been reading, full of brave people, suffering terrible tragedies and injustices but still fighting anyway. Well, it was our duty to help those weaker. Here was our chance, not only to be noble, but to do the right thing.

'His eyes are sad,' Nat added softly. He stroked Pal's arm, but Pal didn't look like he knew anyone was there. 'Don't be sad, fella, I can show you my magic.'

Pal's eyes glittered briefly at that.

'But ...' Arlene shook her head, worried. 'I don't ...' Biting her lip, she twisted her hands. 'Maybe someone else is on their way to help. Might be best if we just ... leave him alone?'

I knew she was worried, but she wasn't thinking straight. The cairn was deserted, except for us. No one was coming to help him.

'I don't think ...' I stopped. What *did* I think? I only knew that I didn't want to send this poor, beaten-up man on his way. What if he had no one and nowhere to go?

'If he wanders off down the village, to them lot, then we'll lose him to the ... you know ... System.'

Arlene's eyes widened. 'What's *the System*?'

'Being abandoned to the System is a fate worse than death,' I said grimly.

'Why?' Arlene asked, tugging at my sleeve. 'What *is* it?'

I only knew bits and pieces. 'It's when you got no say in anything that happens to you. When the bobbies and social workers and ...' I flapped my arms around, trying to find the right words. 'When the busybodies who think they know best start ... meddling.'

Arlene's eyes grew wider, and she nodded solemnly. 'We definitely don't want that, do we?'

'No!' Nat exclaimed.

'It's not just that though, is it, H?' said Lloyd softly, appearing right behind me. He'd taken to calling me H lately. I hadn't told him not to; I liked having a nickname. It felt . . . special. Like a safe secret between us.

As he gazed at Pal, I knew he saw his beloved grampy: games of chess and Airfix models and banjo playing. And there was something about Pal that I trusted, something I felt in my bones – the way he spoke, how he carried himself, the depths in his eyes. I could feel how much he'd seen and I knew Lloyd did too.

I said, 'Let's bring him to Fablehouse. I know where he'll be safe. We can put him up in them old stables.'

'Yeah, no one goes in there. I'll be lookout!' Nat cried, his eyes still on Pal. 'We can feed him till he's all better.'

I turned to Lloyd, but he'd walked away towards the cliff edge and was staring over at the churning wild sea below. I went to him, leaving Arlene and Nat fussing over Pal.

'We can help him, can't we?' I asked.

He didn't look at me. 'H, this is serious.'

'I know.'

'It's not a game,' he said, scuffing the ground. Stones fell over the edge and plummeted down the cliffs. 'He's a real person, and we don't know who he is or where he's come from.'

Churning started in my stomach; I was getting impatient now. 'I *know*.'

I thought we'd already decided this. But no, now here Lloyd was, doing that thing he did, flim-flamming, worrying about being caught and getting into trouble. Trying to dot the *i*'s and cross those *t*'s . . . but sometimes there wasn't certainty. Sometimes you had to abandon all thinking and go with the *feeling*. Sometimes there were no words, nor explaining to be done, you just had to be still; to feel the hairs on your arms shiver up, and the heat flaring in the back of your eyes, and your throat getting squeezed. Sometimes our brains got bogged down in a maze of thoughts, but our bodies gave us clues – I knew that; why didn't Lloyd?

He said evenly, 'What if he's an escaped criminal?'

'An' what if he's not?' I countered.

I thought Lloyd and me were on the same side, that he saw into my heart. I needed him to trust me, to feel what I felt, *to feel the same*, but I couldn't ask him out loud – he had to know it too, really know it, the same as I did.

We stared at each other, unsmiling. Thoughts swirled back and forth between us, me searching his eyes, and him blinking evenly into mine, until the squawk of a bird brought us out of our daze.

'Arlene and Nat need to be safe,' Lloyd said firmly.

'Of course,' I replied softly.

'We have to look out for each other.' He held out his hand, waggling his little finger. 'Pinky promise?'

I linked my little finger with his and, grinning, we squeezed. Lloyd knew as well as I did that we had to protect this stranger. It didn't really matter if our decision was about the System or about us; it was one and the same. The System had abandoned us, but now we had a choice, and no way would we abandon Pal to the same fate.

'All right then,' he said finally, chewing his lip.

In the distance a fox started screaming. I shivered. Something like a heaviness, a force, a rolling heat coming in off the sea, from the trees, was in the air. I didn't know how to explain it, but something somewhere had disturbed the balance of things. We needed to move.

We walked back to Pal. Lloyd came around to his other side and we knelt, holding out our hands for him to take. I gently took Pal's scuffed palm; blood mixed with earth. He stared at my hand blankly. A cloud went over the sun and blotted out the brightness. I shivered again, suddenly cold.

'I'm Heather.'

'Heather,' he repeated, his eyes flickering to life. Amber sparks mingled with the deep brown.

'I'm Lloyd,' Lloyd said, indicating himself as we hauled Pal to his feet. 'We're the Roamers. We'll look after you.'

Chapter Five

The Legend

Pal didn't say much on the way back. We were all quiet as we left the cairn, each of us deep in our own thoughts. Me and Lloyd, without needing to say anything, walked either side of Pal, arms tensed every time he stumbled in case we needed to catch him or help him get his balance. With each of us wheeling a bike too, it was slow going.

Arlene led the way, singing and humming softly while pushing her bike, and Nat pretty much skipped on ahead and around us, whacking at the bristly gorse and ferns with a big branch he'd picked up – making sure Pal didn't rip up his legs where his trousers were torn.

'Careful, mister,' he'd say, and, 'Watch out, brambles about!'

Pal's face was so smooth and curious. Each step we walked, he'd stop and gaze at his surroundings, his eyebrows dancing. He muttered low and under his breath, and I strained to hear his words but couldn't. His eyes brightened when we came to an open space covered in heather and tiny yellow flowers.

We bumped our bikes down the dirt path, exposed up here on the common. I had an uncomfortable sensation of being watched from the dip on the heath. Lloyd too seemed to slow down his steps, and cast a watchful eye around us.

Nearer Fablehouse, Nat, never backward in coming forward, threaded his arm through Pal's and pulled him ahead while he jabbered away, quite excitedly, bobbing through the bracken.

The rest of us wheeled the three bikes carefully behind them both. The weather had cooled quickly, and I winced, noticing two ravens on a branch fighting over the remains of another, smaller bird whose wing was broken. Nature could be so cruel.

Lloyd said, 'It'll be supper soon, and then after that, bath and radio time.'

Arlene muttered as she snagged her stockings on the bicycle chain.

'Ugh! I'm all oily now,' she grumbled, tears filling her eyes. She stopped and glared at the chain as if waiting for it to apologise.

I was about to tell her to not overreact – something an old headmistress always used to say to me: 'Heather, for goodness sake, stop being so ... *dramatic!*' – when I thought better of it. Even though she loved to look her best, Arlene's tears probably weren't about her stockings, were they? Sometimes we cried over the silly stuff cos we couldn't find the right words about what was really bothering us.

Maybe she was frightened about a grown-up finding Pal and us getting into trouble. This was a big thing we'd done, and Lloyd was right – it was serious.

I moved alongside to gently take her bike while she bent over and, sniffing, unhooked her now laddered stocking from the spoke. She smiled gratefully as I passed her bike back. Hopping on it, she pedalled off after Pal and Nat.

I caught up with Lloyd. He walked slowly, eyebrows knitted together with worry. I knew exactly what was on his mind.

'We *are* doing the right thing,' I said, quietly enough that Arlene didn't hear but firmly enough that it didn't appear to be the question that it really was.

'Look how happy Nat is!' Lloyd pointed at Nat's skipping steps as he tried to keep up with Pal's staggering strides. 'He's really taken to him, hasn't he?'

I nodded. 'He has.' I cleared my throat. 'I hope he's not too upset when Pal has to . . . you know, leave.'

Lloyd and I stared at each other, knowing how this would break Nat. Miss Isolde told Lloyd once of how, when Nat was younger, he'd ask any man who came to Fablehouse if he was his father. Miss Isolde said that at first they thought it funny, but then realised how awfully sad it was.

Were we making a mistake, bringing Pal to Fablehouse?

I gestured towards Pal's back. 'Are we being stupid?'

'I don't think so, H,' Lloyd said, glancing sidelong at me, his deep brown eyes steady yet hesitant. 'But I do wonder . . .'

'What?' I said sharply. Why did he look so nervous? 'Wonder what?' He *was* having second thoughts ... I knew it. Why was he wimping out on me? Why couldn't he just make a flippin' decision and stick to it! It was like he didn't even know his own mind half the time. You don't go back on stuff. You don't break promises.

'We could tell Miss Isolde, and then maybe ...' He carried on walking and wheeling, not meeting my eyes.

'No way we're telling any grown-ups!' I yelled, a bit louder than I'd meant to.

'She'll understand. She's very—'

'I don't care!' I couldn't help my voice getting louder. I dropped my bicycle, which clattered, and Pal and Nat up ahead turned round at the noise. Lloyd's words dried on his lips off the glare I fired at him.

I practically barked. 'I *know* she's one of the good ones, but it doesn't matter, does it? She's still a *grown-up*. She'll have to do the right thing, which will be sending him away from us. She'll tell people and make it all ... official.'

'But an adult should know, in case anything goes wrong,' he said quietly.

'No one else will understand. It has to be only Roamers' business!'

Lloyd stared straight ahead, lips pressed together, deep in thought.

The wind had died down, and now everything was utterly still; as if time itself had stopped. Trees weren't swaying. The clouds weren't moving. I couldn't hear any birds, and a chill fell across my shoulders.

'You don't always have to be so … *proper* about everything!' I shouted at Lloyd. 'Don't you *feel* it? How we gotta help him? It's like … it's like he's been given to us!'

Lloyd stared at me, head tilted, that endlessly patient look on his face.

'H, why are you so … cross?'

'I'm not!'

'Well, a lot of the time you act like you are!'

'You don't know nothing!'

But he was right. Now that we were nearer Fablehouse and further away from the cairn, it was as if all my fears and frustrations were bubbling up and spilling over. I don't know why I was so annoyed, but I was.

'You don't have to yell at me just because I don't

agree with you,' Lloyd said, his eyes flashing dark. 'And ...' He closed his eyes, stopping himself from saying anything more.

'Go on, got something else to say?' I asked, arms folded across my chest, waiting. When would he learn to say the truth of what he felt? Why did he always hold back?

He cleared his throat. 'You don't have to say everything that comes into your head; sometimes it's good to be quiet. No harm ever came from thinking before you speak.'

'You sound just like an old man!' I roared.

Silence.

'Sorry,' I said, remembering that he had lived with his grampy.

Lloyd didn't reply. I dug my fingernails into my palms. Finally I said, 'Thinking ... before you speak. Is that what you do?'

He nodded.

'Isn't that hard?' I asked.

'Sometimes.' He sighed heavily. 'But also ... it gives me time to think. You know I don't like breaking the rules. They exist for a reason.'

I wasn't so sure about *that*.

'But ain't this life taught you nothing?'

'What do you mean?'

I threw up my hands, exasperated. 'Being good isn't the same as being *safe*, you know.'

He sighed. 'H, I just want to make sure we're doing the right thing.'

'But maybe sometimes we can't know what that is! We don't always get what we deserve. Bad things happen to good people all the time – look at your grampy and my mum. Stuff ain't fair and that's just life.'

I had to stop speaking then because my throat was doing that thing where the words get tangled and mangled and ached coming out; it felt like I couldn't breathe.

Lloyd looked at me for the longest time. His eyes sort of softened, crinkling round the edges.

'I suppose, if we're helping him, then . . .' His eyes burned through me, and I focused on one thought with all my might, really focused, repeating over and over, *Please trust me, Lloyd, please trust me*, and then . . .

'All right, H. I got it. No telling anyone. No grown-ups. Just us.'

'No grown-ups,' Arlene trilled, turning back to smile at us. 'Just us.' She cycled away again, adding a melody, 'No grown-ups, just us', over and over.

As our bike wheels collected mud and little stones, twigs crunched under our feet, and just for a moment I couldn't shake the image of tiny ancient bones underfoot snapping.

* * *

Nat, Pal and Arlene were waiting for us under cover of the huge oak that stood proudly on the edges of the grounds, to one side of the old caretakers' cottage.

I said, 'If you two go back inside, me and Lloyd will get Pal set up in the stables.'

'Aww!' complained Nat. 'But I wanna help with Pal.'

'I know. But we really need you to – what do they call it? Buy us some time, OK?' I gave him my best *You're really not missing out* smile.

'Why do you get to have all the fun?' Arlene pouted.

'It'll be better if . . . you go and charm Miss Gloria. Please? Tell her me and Lloyd are packing the bikes away.'

I shooed them off and they reluctantly headed up the big lawn towards the house. Pal squinted at the house with curiosity, and pointed, his fingers shaking.

'You'll get spotted.' I pushed his arm down. 'Careful!'

'What fortress is this?' Pal asked, wonder and confusion crossing his face.

'It's home,' Lloyd said, smiling at him.

'That's Fablehouse,' I added. 'It's where we live.'

Pal's gaze roamed over the big, long, yellow building. He took in the sweep of the chimneys and the many windows and doors.

'You are from noble people?' He glanced at our grubby faces with disbelief.

The words he used, and his slow, deliberate way of speaking, made me think of another time and place somehow.

'C'mon. Let's get you away from where anyone might see you. Come with us.'

We followed the gravel path round the side to the old stables. The stables were damp and housed spiders, earwigs, and heaps of rotten straw, so no one really went in there; it would be the safest place for Pal to spend a few days while we figured out what to do.

Lloyd worked the old water pump next to the rusty troughs while Pal leaned against the stable wall.

'Here, Pal.'

I cupped my hands together, mimed drinking from them and motioned towards Pal. He bent over and tried lapping at the pump's spout.

'Steady on!'

As Pal guzzled, water splashed all over him, but he managed to swallow a few mouthfuls too.

With his shoulder, Lloyd barged open the rickety stable door; Pal looked like he was hanging off his hinges too, ready to drop. His face was ashy, chalky, and the glow had gone from behind his eyes. Lloyd and I took an arm each and gently tried to lower him down – though really, he half fell – into a massive pile of dry and dusty straw in one corner.

'Wait here, you'll be able to rest soon,' I said.

He turned his face to me and smiled, or tried to, but his lips trembled. What did he need? How could we help him? What if he needed a real doctor?

'Refreshment . . .' he croaked.

Lloyd looked to me. 'That's right! Food. He must be starving. We can bring him something, can't we?'

'But we can't go to the kitchens now. Let's wait till supper, then we can fill our pockets. And, if we all do it – he should have enough to keep him going.'

Lloyd nodded. 'But we can't stay here with him, can we? Everyone will wonder where we've got to.'

He was right. Mornings would be trickiest. If the four of us kept disappearing in between when we were supposed to be collecting eggs, cleaning out the chickens or being in our lessons, then suspicions would quickly be raised.

'We'll just be careful. Take it in shifts looking after him,' I said.

While Pal caught his breath, Lloyd looked in the storeroom at the back for anything useful. I found a ladder and, together, we leaned it against the entrance to the loft area. If anyone apart from us happened to come into the old stables, even if Pal was sitting up, he wouldn't be easily spotted.

'Pal?' I knelt and shook him. He'd slumped over, eyes closed. I bit my lip, my heart banging. Lloyd stood by, keeping an eye on the doors.

'Pal?' My voice broke, and as it did, Pal's eyes fluttered. He took a moment to focus and then stared at me.

'Listen. To be properly safe, you'll need to climb. Think you can do that?'

He tilted his face upwards. Lloyd and I watched carefully. Was he all right? Could he understand us? He held out his hands. Lloyd and I gripped one each and helped him to his feet. He weighed a ton; it was as if he were carved out of granite; like the cairn – forever here.

'Show me the quest!' he said, his voice booming through the stale stillness of the stables.

I stifled a giggle. 'More like a ladder . . .'

We guided Pal over to the ladder and held either side while he gingerly climbed. I sighed in relief seeing the rungs hold his weight. Once at the top, he rolled on to his stomach and peered down over the edge at the two of us.

Just for a moment I recognised something in his expression, in his flickering eyes. I swallowed a thickness in my throat against it: he was frightened. *Poor Pal.*

No wonder. He didn't know where or who he was and had no idea yet if we were friends or foe. I'd felt like this many times – whatever age you were, fear and loneliness struck the same, didn't it?

And he must be so far from home.

'Pal,' I whispered, tilting my neck to look up at him. 'Stay here. You'll be safe, I promise.'

The minute I made the promise I hoped it would be true and that we could all keep it. I'd do anything not to let him down.

Lloyd had found a pair of old caretaker's overalls in the storeroom, and he tossed them up to Pal.

'Try these – least they're not ripped,' Lloyd called up. They'd barely cover his shins, but it was better than him staying in his tattered smock.

'We'll come back soon, and then ...' I stared at Lloyd and shrugged. Because ... and then? And then what?

Lloyd said firmly, 'And then Heather and me will think of a plan to get you home.'

He sounded so sure of himself that even I believed him. Of course that was what we were going to do; we could do this.

I moved the ladder away so that no one else could get up. 'We will look after you.'

Us Roamers would get Pal wherever he belonged.

Chapter Six

A Man of Mystery

I should have known better than to tell Nat and Arlene to sneak as much food as possible into their pockets without making it obvious, because come supper time, Nat came down wearing his outdoor coat.

As usual, the dining room was noisy with the rowdiness of thirteen children. Miss Isolde, at the head of the table, had her eyes closed and was massaging her fingers to her temples. Everyone was probably giving her a headache, although normally she'd laugh and joke along, but it had been a scorching afternoon and everyone looked a little sunburnt and frazzled. The younger ones made a right mess with their mashed potato. Henry and Michael had stacked sliced carrots into tall piles and were trying to knock each other's down while Leon and Ruth flicked peas at one another across the table.

Miss Gloria sat next to Judy, trying to get her to eat. Judy had her mouth firmly clamped shut, shaking her head.

'Come on, sweetie.' Miss Gloria manoeuvred a spoon near her lips. 'You've not eaten all day, but it's liver and bacon, your favourite!'

Judy growled and folded her arms. Glaring, she turned away from Miss Gloria and whispered in Jeremiah's ear instead. Sighing, Miss Gloria turned her focus to Nat instead.

'And what, young man, may I ask is that you're wearing?'

Nat got all flustered – bless him, he can't lie for toffee – and mumbled about being cold.

'Cold?' barked Miss Isolde, opening her eyes, incredulous. 'Nathaniel, it's a perfectly balmy summer evening.'

Nat coughed and blushed. 'But I weren't feeling good.'

Miss Isolde peered at him, unblinking. 'I suggest you pay a visit to sick bay after supper then; we'll dose you up with some castor oil and before you know it, you'll be right as rain.'

Castor oil! That sticky gloop was the worst!

I thought she was joking, but there was no smile – her face was pinched tight. She kept absent-mindedly spinning her purple ring and I noticed that underneath, the skin was blistered and chapped.

'Unless, of course, you'd like to remove your overcoat at the supper table?' Miss Isolde carried on, peering at him.

Nat glanced at me with raised eyebrows and a *What should I do?* expression, so I mimed taking the coat off.

And with that, Nat took his coat right off.

* * *

Later, Lloyd kept watch while I snuck into the cupboards above the pantry. We could hardly take Pal liver and bacon, mash and carrots, could we? So I rooted around for a crust of bread, slices of ham, a hunk of cheese and an apple. Iodine – good for cuts – was kept there too. Then all four of us headed out to the stables.

One by one we climbed the ladder. In the loft, Pal was huddled over, hugging his knees and shivering slightly, but he'd changed into the overalls.

'We've brought food!' Lloyd said brightly. He took off his jacket and laid it out like a tablecloth. I emptied my pockets and grinned at our haul; we'd done all right. Lloyd had also swiped a bottle which we'd filled with sweet tea, cold now but still good.

We sat there, cross-legged, watching Pal tuck into the food, eating as if he hadn't done for days. Flecks of breadcrumbs flew from his lips as he tore the crust into smaller chunks. His hair ropes swung back and forth.

'Samson had long hair, didn't he?' Arlene said, staring at them, fascinated. 'He was very strong.'

'You spoke of magic?' Pal stopped to turn and stare at Nat. 'What is this magic of which you speak?'

'Oh, didn't you know?' Arlene beamed. 'Our Nat fancies himself a magician, he's got really good lately.'

'*Fancies*?!' Nat puffed out his chest. 'My magic is as real as the nose on your face, if you don't mind!'

Pal's thick eyebrows knitted together. 'What magic do you . . .'

Nat rummaged in his pockets and brought out two coins. 'Watch carefully!' he said, then proceeded to spin them round. 'Now, I'll make this coin disappear before your very eyes!'

Pal shifted forward, eyes fixed on Nat's hands, as he moved them around quickly back and forth.

'Where have the coins gone?' Nat crowed, opening his empty hands.

Pal suddenly stood up. 'Where have you vanquished them to?' He sounded aghast, and reached for one of Nat's hands, opening the fingers, as if he expected to find the coins there.

Nat sniggered. 'A magician never tells!'

Pal sank back, breathing heavily. His smile had vanished and his cheeks looked sunken. Disappointed, he focused on biting into his apple.

After Pal had finished eating, I said, 'This might sting, but it'll help,' and using the edge of my sleeve, I dabbed at some of his cuts and scratches with the iodine. Nat squeezed Pal's fingers while he flinched. Arlene sang softly about gladness and sadness and tears being near, and beamed when Pal nodded along to her singing.

'This will take your mind off the pain too.' Lloyd brought out his bundle of cigarette cards that he always kept in his top shirt pocket. 'Look at my latest!'

He shifted closer and unwrapped the elastic band holding the thick pack of small cards together. The staff brought in the cards – they came free with cigarette packs or tea boxes.

'What is that?' Pal pointed to the card Lloyd had passed to him.

'A cigarette card,' Lloyd said proudly. 'I collect them. This series is about birds.'

I glanced at the birds' beautiful colours and flipped the card over to read the information on the back. 'This is a falcon.' I pointed to the card as Pal gingerly held it between his fingers.

He frowned. 'What is a cigarette card?' He sniffed it and squinted at the tiny print on the back. 'A magical emblem?' He looked at us, confusion all over his face.

Lloyd and I stared at each other, worried. Pal must have taken a bigger beating than we'd thought, especially if it was affecting his memory.

'I can ...' Lloyd closed his eyes briefly before

taking a big breath. 'I can leave these with you if you'd like something to look at,' he said kindly, handing his precious cards over. My heart ballooned with pride for my friend, knowing how much it took for him to hand those over. The little rectangular cards looked tiny in Pal's massive hands. Even if he didn't quite know what they were, he knew they were special to Lloyd.

'Thank you for entrusting these to me. I will guard them with my life.'

'I can show you my marbles tomorrow!' Nat said, excited.

'And I've got a book with all the movie stars in,' Arlene added.

I felt bad now that I'd not brought anything, but then an image of knights head to toe in shiny silver armour charging on horseback thundered through my mind – I could show Pal my Dead Arthur book tomorrow! Who wouldn't love those adventures?

'We'd better go now,' I said. 'We listen to the wireless over hot milk and toast before bedtime, and if we ain't there – people's tongues might start wagging.'

Pal looked quizzical. 'The . . . ?'

'The wireless.'

Pal's face, once again, was blank. He had no idea what I was talking about. Maybe he didn't have cigarette cards or a wireless where he was from? But what sort of place was that? Suddenly I felt like a balloon that had popped, and our promise to help struck me as impossible.

'So, have you not remembered *anything*?' Arlene asked, plucking at the straw around Pal's feet, sighing dramatically. 'The food must have made you feel better, more yourself?'

He touched his fingers to his dry lips, brow creased. 'Amorrow ... a voyage.' He spoke hesitantly, as if just waking up.

Lloyd sat up straighter. 'Anything else?'

It clearly took Pal great effort, straining to capture his thoughts. 'I travelled great distances, tasked with an important ...' Pal's gaze landed on Nat, and he pointed at him, waving his hands. 'You! You spoke of magic, and I too feel I know a little of this, but ...' He shook his head, frustrated, frowning. 'My mind is a dark cloud, veiled over ...'

I knew that feeling ... of trying to grasp a

thought or dream that you could hardly remember. Probably how my mother felt, when the madness chewed her up from inside, and how Lloyd's grampy felt, trying to keep a hold of himself.

'The land holds a familiar scent ... like soil after rain. The roots holding on, through the earth. I recognise it, but underneath is a stench I know to fear, yet the particulars ... they elude me.'

Us Roamers had promised to help this man, this stranger, but he was so lost and confused. Perhaps we couldn't turn back now, but who was he really? Where had he come from, and what was he doing here?

He was far from ordinary, that much was clear.

Chapter Seven

Fun and Games

I read Dead Arthur late into the night, aided by a torch, but my sleep was fitful. I woke three or four times; each time, I'd booted my blankets off and was sweating, as if I'd been running.

Now, at the breakfast table, I chewed a thick mouthful of porridge before pulling a face.

'Eww!' I spat lumps of porridge out on to my side plate.

Martha, who could always be relied upon to comment on everything, called out, rather meanly, 'Add salt instead of sugar again?'

'No!' I poked my tongue out. 'The cream has curdled.'

At the end of the table sat Jeremiah and Judy, sniggering. Judy made jerky signs with her hands, waiting for Jeremiah to copy her.

'I'll tell Cook.' Arlene picked up the jug, sniffed it and wrinkled her nose. 'Smells horrible!' She disappeared through the doors which led into the kitchen.

'Where's Miss Isolde?' I asked Martha.

Martha cracked her hard-boiled egg and sniffed. 'Miss Betty says she's not feelin' well. Resting in her office and she's not to be disturbed, so I heard.'

The grandfather clock chimed louder than usual, startling us all.

Lloyd glanced at the younger ones and, lowering his voice, said, 'I snuck out earlier and gave Pal an apple, but it's no good, him being cooped up in the stables. He needs to get some fresh air.' He took two slices of bread from the rack and laid them on his plate.

Arlene came back and set down a fresh jug of cream. 'Cook says sorry, she doesn't know what's up with the milk and cream this week. She thinks, because it's so hot, that everything's going off quicker.'

I frowned at her. 'But last night there was a big rain shower!'

Nat slid the butter dish down to Lloyd. 'Let's take Pal to the lake!' He leaned back in his chair. 'I can show Pal how to skim stones. I can do four skips in a row now!'

Sitting next to Nat, Arlene nudged him gently in the ribs. 'It's not all about you, you know.' She tossed her pigtails, making me want to add, 'An' it's not all about you neither,' but I didn't.

There was plenty of Pal to go around. And there was no point us bickering. This was about us finding out where Pal should be, and who he belonged to. Even though none of us had any clue how to do that, we knew what it was like to not have a home, to feel out of place and that you didn't belong. Poor Pal. He had been dressed like a wanderer – what must it be like for him, travelling around unfamiliar places and trying to settle down? Maybe all while his real home and hearth pulled at his heart. We all knew how tough that was.

Maybe Lloyd was right and being cooped up wasn't good for Pal. Maybe a change of scene would jog his memory and give us a clue on how to help him.

'The lake?' I said, smiling at Nat. 'It *is* Saturday.'

Saturdays were bliss – no lessons, freedom to come and go as we pleased, apart from mealtimes, and no church neither.

'We could ask for a picnic!' Arlene exclaimed. 'Couldn't we, Lloyd? If we help with extra chores after breakfast, Miss Gloria will say yes, I just know it!' She clapped her hands together excitedly. 'They like us not gettin' under their feet, don't they?'

* * *

Lloyd piled on the charm and Miss Gloria agreed that we could take a picnic on our day out 'exploring'.

From the lawn, I noticed Miss Isolde's office curtains were drawn, and staff were in the pantry gathering cleaning supplies; there wasn't a better time to get Pal away from prying eyes.

Nat kept lookout while Arlene and I strapped the wicker picnic hamper to the back of Lloyd's bicycle. The day was sunny and clear with a light breeze, and my heart felt light. I'd packed my Dead Arthur book to show Pal.

We'd agreed to only take one bike since the lake wasn't too far.

Lloyd had gone on ahead and snuck into the stables to help Pal down. Seeing him walk towards us without limping made my already good mood even better. His cuts and scratches had dried up and the swelling had gone down, though he'd be left with some impressive bruises, that much was clear.

'Now where are you young ones taking me?' Pal asked, arm loose round Lloyd's shoulder.

'A lake's nearby,' I said. 'Much closer than the cairn. Maybe you'll see something you recognise if you live round here?'

'A good idea.' Pal smiled, although he looked slightly sad. 'Perhaps the scenery will stir my spirit enough to remember.'

'There's ducks at the lake!' Nat said.

As we walked, following the narrow path that led to the lake half a mile away, Pal's eyes lit up, the golden flecks dancing round the irises. He scanned the hedges and bushes we passed, eyes darting high and low.

'Do you know the plants which can help you?'

'Yes. Miss Isolde teaches us about that,' I said.

'Miss . . . ?'

'Isolde. She's our headmistress.'

'Isolde. Hmn.' Pal's brow furrowed as if the name were familiar to him. 'You do well to be taught by scholars who understand the land. I would benefit from finding some woundwort.' He put his hands on his knees and crouched.

'Why d'ya need that?' Nat asked, as we examined the hedgerows. 'What is it?'

'Woundwort is a plant with dark green feathery leaves and small white flowers clustered tightly together. It stems bleeding. And who knows what battles one may have to face in future days.' Pal stopped to retie his hair ropes, which were swinging loose around his shoulders.

'Aha!' he cried, tugging at a bunch of green leaves from low in the hedges. 'This shall do nicely!' He held his hand tight over the leaves on his arm.

"Effver! Heffver!'

Behind us chirruped a familiar voice. I whirled round to face Davey barrelling up the lanes, panting, holding his flat cap on with one hand.

'Davey!' *Now what?* We'd come too far to go back but ... 'You shouldn't be out here on your own!'

'I'll be good. I promise!' he beseeched. 'Miss Betty an' Miss Clara is too busy for games.' He held out his arms. 'Carry me!'

I sighed and bent down so that he could hop on my back. 'Don't squeeze too tight, all right?'

Nat, Arlene and Lloyd stared at Davey openmouthed, terrified. They tried to shield Pal from view, which was pointless, since Pal towered over all of us.

'Hullo, mister!' Davey said brightly, waving at Pal; not fazed in the slightest, as if seeing a dark-skinned man like him were a regular sight.

'Hullo, young man,' Pal replied. 'Pleased to meet you. I like your hat.'

'Ta!' Davey tipped his cap at him, started humming and didn't give Pal another glance, although I knew us Roamers' hearts were in our throats.

As I drew alongside Lloyd, Davey sniffed and pointed to the hamper strapped to the back of the bike.

"S'there 'nuff food for me?'

Lloyd nodded. 'Absolutely. Miss Gloria packs enough grub for an army; there'll be plenty.'

'An army?' Pal faltered, stopping and peering at Lloyd strangely.

Lloyd smiled. 'Oh, don't worry – it's just a turn of phrase, Pal.'

Arlene and Nat walked ahead with Pal, and Lloyd whistled quietly as he pushed his bike. Davey and I brought up the rear, with Davey giggling and reaching up for the tree branches we passed.

When the tree-lined path ended, it curved around and opened out on to a copse at the edge of the lake.

Seeing the lake again, its beauty sent shivers down my arms. With the sun high in the sky now, shafts of sunlight tunnelled down, dazzling on the gently shifting glassy surface. On a day like today, it took your breath away to see such stillness. It felt as if everything inside me lapped quiet.

'Magnificent!' Pal breathed deeply, taking it in. 'Being out in the world is balm for the soul.'

It was indeed.

I looked into his wide and shining eyes. He looked well for the first time since we'd found him; rested and happy.

'Can we eat now?' Davey begged, as he wriggled down off my back. 'My tummy's rumblin'!'

Lloyd unstrapped the hamper while I held his

bike. He set the hamper on the ground while Arlene unpacked a checked blanket and shook it out.

Sitting on the blanket, I carefully opened the bundles Miss Gloria had packed; heaps of food tumbled out between folded napkins – slabs of buttered crusty bread, hard-boiled eggs, and thick slices of pink ham. Apples, oranges and plums, as well as fruit cake, ginger cake, and currant buns wrapped up in newspaper. There was a bottle of home-made lemonade and a bottle of ginger beer to drink too.

Pal watched me eagerly as I picked up an orange. I handed him one and he bit into it before recoiling and spitting out the peel.

I laughed. 'No, like this.' I demonstrated, curling a length of peel round my fingers. He inhaled deeply, beaming. Then he tore the orange in half and shoved his face into it, slurping noisily. Orange juice ran down his chin and we laughed so much that I got a stitch.

'Such sticky nectar.' Pal licked his fingers and wiped at his chin. 'Now I will try this.' He reached over and separated two slices of bread stuck together. He sniffed the dark sticky spread before taking a bite.

Closing his eyes, he chewed slowly, and then licked his lips.

'Mmn, what is this delicious fare?'

Nat, trying his best to scoff an entire egg, peered at the crust Pal had left. 'Eww. That's Marmite – you like it? Miss Betty is crazy for it.'

'It is very good indeed!' He beamed. 'Rich and beefy.'

We stared at him, disgusted. None of us liked Marmite, although Miss Betty kept trying to force it on us at every opportunity, saying how it was packed full of vitamins. As if that would make any of us try it!

I made myself a sandwich of ham and egg and washed it down with ginger beer.

Dusting breadcrumbs from his lap, Pal rubbed his belly and leaned back on his elbows. 'Tell me, has there ever been such a feast as this?'

'Yes!' Nat hiccupped and covered his mouth. 'Christmas at Fablehouse is the best, specially when it snows. There's sledding and carols and chocolate and stockings!'

Christmas. I'd never really had a nice Christmas. Probably because I was born on 20th December, and Mum was always extra sad around that time.

'The best time I ever had was at the Saturday morning pictures.' Arlene rolled up her slice of ham, nibbling it round the edges.

'I've never been to the picture palace,' Nat said. 'Isn't sitting in the dark scary?'

Arlene shook her head. 'Oh, no. It's cosy. A thick red curtain opens at the front and the screen is a hundred times bigger than any television.' Hands clasped together, she stared rapturously into the clouds as if seeing the moving images above her.

I'd never been to the pictures either. Couldn't imagine sitting in the darkness, staring at people playing make-believe. I liked reading, or listening to the radio, where I could imagine the pictures for myself.

'*Singing in the Rain* was the best, but I loved *Peter Pan* too.' Arlene sighed, plucked at the long grass by her feet. 'Mum met my dad at the pictures. She took me all the time. When the film finished, she'd sit there for ages, sniffing in the dark. She thought I didn't know she was crying; but I did. When we got home, she'd go straight to bed, even though it was daytime. I had to get me own lunch and supper.'

Arlene had a photo of her mother on her bedside cabinet: she could have been a movie star herself. And, not for the first time, I wondered what the truth of Arlene's own story really was.

'Why did she like sad films?' Nat asked, scrunching up his nose.

Arlene shook her head. 'They wasn't sad films. She'd go and watch anything; sometimes went twice in one day. That's one reason I got brought here. Mum went to the picture house and three days later, she hadn't come back. Neighbours found me on my own.'

Silence fell over us then. A silence where I knew we were all thinking of home, where that was and what it meant.

Arlene picked at a slice of fruit cake. Nat and Lloyd played rock, paper, scissors. Davey was curled up, snoring softly. We gazed across the lake, the wind gently rippling the surface of the water. I squinted – my eyes playing tricks. For a moment I thought I saw fingertips poking up through the water, but it was just the willows and reeds.

Pal licked the ginger-cake stickiness off his fingers. 'A feast fit for a king ...' As he said the word 'king', he recoiled, suddenly confused, but then shook his head. 'After food, entertainment is traditional!'

'I could read?' I said, suddenly a little shy. 'I brought my storybook. There's a lady in a lake who gives a special sword to this boy.'

Pal gasped. 'Arthur?'

Suddenly his eyes dulled, and he fell to muttering. We looked at him, a little concerned.

Eventually he rubbed his chin. 'A lady in a lake, you say?'

I nodded. 'Oh, they're grand adventures! You'll love them, I'm sure.'

'Indeed.' Pal folded his hands over his stomach. 'That would suit very much, young miss.' His eyes searched mine.

I went to the hamper and brought out the book. I turned to the story about the Lady of the Lake. As I read aloud about Arthur and Merlin climbing down off their horses and taking the sword from the water, Pal leaned forward, hands scrunched into fists, mouth half open, hanging on to every word.

'These aren't stories! I have lived these tales. I know of Arthur. He was ... he is *my* king!' Pal's eyes flashed with recognition. 'Let me look upon those pages!' The sun burst out, lighting him up, the silver birches rustling. I passed the book to him. Pal's fingers moved across the letters, his expression faraway, as if he heard or saw something that none of us could.

'A king ... Arthur, a sword, a lake. It all makes sense. I know these happenings. But how can they be here? Flat on parchment – stories? These are true adventures I have lived ... battles I have fought!'

He sat up straight and shouted, his voice booming and commanding. 'I remember!' He jumped to his feet. 'I am Palamedes.' His brown eyes gleamed. He thudded a fist to his chest, his hair ropes swaying. 'I am a knight! One of Arthur's knights. I swore to protect him and to stand alongside him, upholding peace throughout the Kingdom of Logres. These lands ...'

'You what?' breathed Nat.

'What are you talking about?' Arlene looked between Nat and Pal, bewildered.

Lloyd and I stared at each other, eyebrows raised and mouths open.

'I swear every word I utter is true. I am a knight. I used to wear shiny silver armour, my sword in its scabbard, astride a fine jet-black horse with sleek skin and a mane to rival my own.'

Pal sounded excited and alive as he spoke, his eyes gleaming, but then, almost as quick, he crumpled like a tower of ash and slumped. He stared at his palms, his breathing ragged.

Again he said, 'I remember,' but this time it was the opposite of how he'd yelled it so triumphantly only a moment before. 'So many of us came and went over the years. Me and my brothers—'

'Brothers?' Lloyd asked.

'You're a *knight*!' Nat's eyes twinkled. 'I *knew* you were the best.'

'I am not the best.' Pal's voice cracked. He put his hand gently on Nat's curls. 'I recall that no one thought me good enough. Even after I fought the Questing Beast . . . I never was considered worthy of eating at the Round Table,' he said quietly. 'King Arthur appointed me himself, centuries ago, but I was not welcomed into the fold. I was never embraced wholeheartedly, and without question, as you young adventurers embrace me now. I had a friend, Mark, a champion, and he promised that we'd fight the Questing Beast together.'

'What's a questing beast?' Arlene breathed, mouth open, as we crowded round him.

'A loathsome creature with the body of a leopard, a serpent's head, a lion's hindquarters, and rabbit's feet. At the time, it was the most fearsome beast known to man, and threatened everything King Arthur's court held dear. A noise, like the barking of a pack of wild hounds, came from its stomach.'

Nat tugged on Pal's sleeve. 'And where is your friend now?'

Pal hung his head sadly. 'He abandoned me at the final battle and left me for dead. The whispers in court were that he had escaped to another realm.'

'What's a realm?' I frowned.

'A world which exists alongside our own.'

Had the sun gone to Pal's head? Surely he meant another country . . .

Lloyd peered closely at Pal, trying to make sense of what he was saying.

'But why—'

'No doubt to bargain for his own gain.'

Pal had been let down and abandoned, just like us. I knew it. 'Why did he go to another place?'

'Because in the realm of Fae he is not only a knight, but able to wield great power. He can command magic from the land. He has unlimited strength. He can move mountains and shape stones, creating pillars from mounds of earth and weaving vines into ropes. Mark can be cruel and cunning. He always craved power and dominion over others.'

Lloyd had started pacing, hands clenched in his hair. 'But, how come you're alive now, it's 1954!'

'I do not know,' Pal said simply, his bushy eyebrows knitted together, deep in thought.

'Knights have quests, don't they?' Nat said. 'Are you on a quest? Maybe you have family waiting?'

We all stopped then. We'd never considered that Pal might have a family, or children like us, eagerly waiting for his return; probably more upset than any of us could imagine.

Davey grunted and rolled over in his sleep. My head was spinning. If Pal wasn't even from this time or place, then how could we help him now? He had – like us – no real home to go back to!

'We'd best head back,' I said coolly, dusting cake crumbs off my lap. I shut the book and put it back in the hamper. I gently shook Davey awake. He yawned, grumbled, and curled up into a ball again. Pal bent over and swept him up in his arms.

'Careful!' Nat said, touching his arm. 'You're still getting better.'

Pal rearranged Davey over his shoulder and smiled softly at Nat. 'I am, that's true.'

Nat chewed his fingernails and said quietly, unable to look at the rest of us, 'So you ain't my father then, are you? I started wondering . . . hoping you was; that you'd come to take me home.' His voice had scraped into a whisper.

Pal gazed into Nat's grubby hopeful little face. 'I am not.' His voice was soft and low. 'But, if I *were* a father, I would be proud to have a son such as you.'

Lloyd and I gasped, a catch in our throats at exactly the same time. Arlene's fingers dropped the daisy chain she'd been making. With Pal's words – for a second – we'd all been transported to alternative lives where we knew our fathers. We knew those brave men who had fought on the right side, for us, and fallen in love whilst doing so. And, just like that, our bond – our love for Pal – was sealed.

Davey wiggled and snuffled on Pal's shoulder. 'Whha?' he mumbled, breaking our spell.

I threw warning glances at the others – we needed to be careful with what we said now, with Davey awake.

'You sure you can manage?' Lloyd asked Pal.

'That woundwort helped what ails me. And I know my identity now; I feel stronger. I am a knight; it is my duty, my purpose, to look after and protect others.'

As we strode across the moorland, glossy brown ponies skittered past. Pal looked after them longingly as they tossed their manes.

'I love horses. Do you miss yours?' Arlene asked, seeing him gaze at the ponies with what looked like love in his eyes.

'Indeed. I had a fine steed.' Pal grimaced as if it pained him to speak. Although he no longer limped, he clearly wasn't back to full strength. 'He never left my side, so loyal and true. If he is nowhere to be found, then a great mischief is at hand.'

Knowing who he was gave Pal new vigour as we threaded through the woods and pathways back to

Fablehouse. The only noise was the squeaking of the bicycle wheels. Pal gazed around him, as if seeing it all anew again.

As we approached the front lawn, we noticed children in small groups spread around, so Lloyd helped Pal into the stables round the back. The rest of us went ahead to be greeted by a concerned Miss Gloria at the front door.

'Oh! There you are!' Seeing Davey, she visibly wilted in relief. 'He was with you the whole time? Oh Heather, me and Miss Betty was worried sick. Miss Isolde was ready to string us up.'

'Sorry,' I mumbled. 'We were too far to turn back.'

Arlene gabbled, 'By the time Davey'd caught up with us . . .'

'We was with the Black Knight,' Davey babbled.

Nat squeaked.

Miss Gloria smiled at us and rolled her eyes. 'You been reading him those King Arthur stories?'

A flush came to my face; Davey had almost given the game away!

'Nothing too grisly, I hope?'

I gulped and smiled weakly.

Miss Isolde appeared in the doorway then, looking very pale. I smiled, but she didn't smile back. Instead, she stepped forward and grabbed Davey's hand.

'Come along.' She pulled him forward into the hallway. 'Being out this late isn't good for young boys.' She didn't look at any of us.

We watched Davey trot along behind Miss Isolde. Miss Gloria's cheeks were flushed, and she muttered, 'Don't none of you trouble Miss Isolde now. She's right under the weather and won't be at supper, so please, everyone on their best behaviour.'

Chapter Eight

The Door

'*H*eather ...' whispered a woman's voice. '*We hear you and the longings of your heart. Come hither, Heather ...*'

'Huh?' I spun furiously in my bed, the blankets getting tangled between my legs. Flapping my feet, I shook off the twisted sheets and then instantly brought my feet back under the covers – it was freezing!

Arlene yawned and turned to face me. 'Heather?'

'Did you hear that?' But even as the question stammered out of my mouth, I realised, by Arlene's blank stare, that she had no idea what I was talking about. I'd been dreaming and what a dream it had been. A woman whispering a promise, an invitation. Who was she?

I tried, but couldn't fall back to sleep – may as well get up. Frost had formed overnight on the inside of our bedroom window – but it was the height of summer! How was that even possible? I couldn't shake the feeling that everything felt odd somehow … If Pal wasn't from our time, then what did that mean for us Roamers? What had shifted in the world so that the past and present had been smashed up against each other?

I dressed quickly, grabbed my Dead Arthur book and trotted downstairs and along the corridor.

At the bottom of the stairs, just before the dining room, was an ornate full-length mirror, the grand-father clock next to it. Checking the time, I blinked suddenly. For a second it seemed as if the hands were moving backwards, but that couldn't be right, could it?

I definitely needed more sleep.

Moving my head to the ticking of the swinging pendulum, I glanced into the mirror and pushed the hair back off my face – my rubber band had snapped again. I did look tired. With one hand, I rubbed my eyes and peered forward, almost touching my nose to my reflection. I jerked back. *What?* When I rubbed my eyes, my reflection hadn't done the same! Well, not at the exact same time anyway. My breathing quickened. Maybe I'd been mistaken. There was only one way to be sure. I licked my finger and smoothed an eyebrow. And again, there it was! My reflection delayed doing the same action. I let out a long slow breath and tried to ignore the pounding in my ears. This didn't make any sense.

I yawned; I had to be the delayed one, that was all there was to it. I was just letting my imagination run away with me; I'd been told *that* before.

I tucked my Dead Arthur book under my arm, planning to read some more while it was quiet, before the breakfast chaos. I wanted to see what else it mentioned about Pal; maybe there'd be hints about his quest, why he was here or how we could help him.

As I entered the dining room, warm comforting smells of honey and cinnamon from the kitchen wafted through the air. Maybe, after breakfast, us Roamers could go back to the lake with Pal. We might even get away with not going to church today; Miss Isolde didn't insist we attend. Although Miss Clara said the younger children enjoyed the Bible stories, I thought they enjoyed the free biscuits more.

Carole, who was seven, and Henry, who was eight, were alone at the table, sitting opposite each other. Strange for them to be up this early, especially with no other staff about, and they weren't the type to wait patiently. Often, Miss Gloria sent me to Carole's room to make sure she didn't miss breakfast, but this morning she sat stiffly, staring right ahead.

'Morning!' I ruffled her hair.

She didn't move, or blink. I leaned forward – was she actually asleep?

'Hi, Henry,' I said, waving at him. He blinked slowly, following my hand. His teeth chattered as if he were very cold.

'You all right? Carole?' I put my hand on her shoulder, shaking it, but she only stared at her plate with no expression.

The longer I stared at them, the eerier I felt. It was like they both had no idea that I was even there.

'Where's Cook?' Taking a seat next to Carole,

I joked, 'Taken a vow of silence or somethin'? That would be a first, eh?'

Henry turned his head and gazed at me, eyes wider than usual and the whites bloodshot. Carole stirred an empty bowl, clutching the spoon so hard that her knuckles paled. I'd never seen either of them like this, so quiet and unresponsive. Under Carole's chin, there was what looked like a hazy green glow. I blinked quickly; I must have been staring too long in one spot.

'Carole?' I reached for her forehead, but she yanked herself back, a sly look swimming into her narrowed eyes.

She sort of ... *hissed* at me! I shivered, creeping coldness fluttering across the back of my neck. I tried to keep my voice cheerful. Maybe they both had too much sun yesterday? Or had eaten something which disagreed with them?

'Hold up and I'll fetch Miss Gloria. She'll sort you out, with a dose of cod liver oil I shouldn't wonder!'

As I stood, Carole's little hand shot out and tight fingers grabbed my wrist.

'No!' she cried, her voice cracking.

'No!' echoed Henry, turning to stare at me.

'There's nothing to be afraid of,' I said. They both sounded strained, as if hands were crushing their throats and 'No' was all they could croak out.

I glanced at Carole's hand, her fingers still wrapped around my wrist, her grip tight. Her fingernails were pointed and sharp and digging into my flesh. Looking directly into her eyes, I gulped. My head started spinning a little. *Carole* felt wrong. This wasn't the Carole I knew. I didn't know how to explain it; this girl looked like Carole but wasn't. Something was *very* wrong.

I started feeling light-headed, so I forced my breath to come even and slow. Like the times I was about to get a smacking, steeling myself against the urge to cry out or run.

I tried to smile, but Carole's contorted face, her sour expression, turned my stomach and I had to look away. I glanced at Henry, panicked, as Judy, Jeremiah, Ruth and Michael came in, bickering loudly. I waited for someone to say something, but they just sat down. Cook burst through the kitchen doors, backwards.

'Morning, all!' she boomed heartily, setting down

racks of toast and bowls of porridge. *Where were the Roamers?*

Everyone calmly ate their porridge. Carole grinned at me, showing a full mouthful of teeth – except they weren't like no teeth I'd ever seen – they were yellow and pointed upside-down jagged triangles!

Don't show you're afraid, don't show you're afraid, chanted my mind like the chorus of a song. Couldn't anyone else see what I saw? My mind whirred into action, my mouth opened, and the words fell out before I had even a chance to consider what I was saying.

'Okey-dokey, Carole,' I said, too loud and too cheerful. 'As long as you feel OK! I better get going – don't want Miss Gloria finding me with that comb of hers.'

Carole's eyes looked glassy. 'Yass,' she said, lisping slightly.

I shoved back my chair and stood, not convinced my knees would hold me, and left the dining room, fear skittering along my spine as the *Carole-not-Carole* images lingered in my mind. Feeling dazed, I walked the corridors of Fablehouse, replaying what I'd seen over and over. If *that* wasn't Carole, then who was it?

I had to find the others and tell them what I'd seen.

* * *

As I headed for the stables, I saw Lloyd, Arlene and Nat outside with Pal.

'You're never going to believe what I've just seen!' I exclaimed.

I explained how odd Carole and Henry had seemed at breakfast, as well as the tricks my eyes had played on me as I'd looked into the mirror.

'Everything here just feels strange,' I finished. 'Something isn't right. Can't you feel it?'

Lloyd said, 'Maybe you caught the sun a bit yesterday?' He cleared his throat, staring at his boots.

'It *was* very hot,' nodded Arlene, flicking Nat a look.

They thought I was being dramatic! Indignation flashed in me. But Pal was staring at me with an intense searching expression, eyebrows creased.

'What is it?' I asked, looking to them all, worried. 'Pal?'

'I have remembered many other elements from my life. What I was doing before you found me. If what I fear has happened and the Fae have breached the cairn ...' His lips trembled; he looked like he was shrinking, the air being sucked out of him.

'What does that mean?' I asked.

'We need to go immediately to where you found me!' Pal said, striding towards the lanes which led to the cairn.

'I should never have left,' he muttered as we raced alongside him. 'Hurry!'

'It's far,' Lloyd said, jogging to catch up with him. 'Let us at least take the bikes.'

'No! Your wheels will make too much noise.'

'Is he all right?' Nat asked, looking at me nervously; I didn't know what to tell him.

We tried to keep up with Pal's strides. Nat hurried alongside him. Breathing heavily, Pal said, 'You sense how special the place is, don't you – those stones infused with wonder?'

'Yes,' we murmured as our feet crunched over the gorse and bracken.

'I know it's magic there,' Nat babbled. 'You can smell it in the air.'

I had no idea what magic smelt like, but we all knew that the cairn affected us, that was undeniable.

I thought of how the stones humming under my fingertips made me feel. A quieting, a settling deep inside, whenever we were within a few feet of them. They affected Arlene too; her tall tales changed into sweet truths, her face softened, and she wasn't bothered if her hair came undone or she spilt something down her pinafore. Nat became calm and less jumpy. And Lloyd laughed more easily as soon as the stones were in sight; he stopped fretting over every little thing – he was able to let go and just *be*.

'You asked how I had come to be here, in this time and place.' Pal closed his eyes as if summoning something from within. 'I remember. I swore to be suspended in time. To guard the doorway between worlds – that is the cairn! But, if I am here with you, and awake, then the spell has been broken.'

He hung his head. 'And if the doorway is open, then we are in mortal danger.' His voice cracked and dried up.

'What do you mean, danger?' asked Arlene, biting her nails.

'Danger from others.'

'Who?' Lloyd demanded.

'Have you ever wondered, "Is this all there is"?' Pal turned to us, his eyes desperate and searching. 'Only man is so vain as to believe he is the only one who inhabits this earth. But there are many worlds unseen and unknown to the human realm.'

Nat piped up, 'I don't understand.'

'An apple has seeds, yes? And inside those seeds is another tree waiting to sprout, another world. Under the cairn, deep in the bowels of the soil, lies another realm: Fae Feld.'

He'd mentioned that word yesterday! But now it felt like he was talking in riddles. I was getting annoyed. 'What's that?' I demanded.

'Where the Fae folk reside.'

'Fae? Like fairies?' Arlene gasped. 'Beautiful, like Tinker Bell, with little wings?'

Pal scratched his head. 'Fae folk are many and varied, as are we. But within Fae there are no wings and no ... wands. They're not human in appearance, thought or deed. They can take any form they wish, blend in or stand out. They are known by many names. Some Fae protect humans, or work with them for the good of the land and society, but other Fae folk . . .'

He trailed off and stared at the ground, deep in thought. 'Others want to threaten the mortal realm. They use their magic for evil, they wish to overthrow humankind.'

'Why do they do that?' Lloyd asked, agitated.

'Many Fae desire power, control. They can be greedy and grasping, desiring gold and riches. Some are tricksters who want to rule the mortal world because they feel mistreated, misunderstood. Over the centuries they were promised things, but not everything went their way. Fae are not permitted to rule over mortals – a world with magic is too dangerous – so they had to make a choice. But there was dissent and factions arose; many deaths and much destruction. And so Merlin banished the Fae to a world beneath ours. But it is a place where warmth is absent; the sun never shines.'

'So how can they get into our world? How does it work?' I asked, terror gripping me at the thought of a threat to Fablehouse and my friends.

'First, they send spies. Changelings sneak into your homes and leave one of their own – they'll look exactly like the person they've stolen; except they are not them, of course. Then they watch and wait, gaining more knowledge of the human world, all the while increasing their power.'

One look at Pal and I knew he was telling us the truth.

I thought of Carole and Henry at breakfast: my insides felt as if I'd swallowed shards of glass.

My stomach lurched. 'And if they've already … replaced you, then what happens?' I stuttered, fearful.

'By then … it's too late, they've crossed the threshold. And if they've done that, it means they have allies of their own.'

'That's stupid.' Arlene sniffed. 'Who'd help the bad guys?'

'Anyone who desires power or riches. It may be difficult for an honest person to understand, but Fae often find humans who are willing to assist them.'

I thought of my mother, who'd once stolen a loaf of bread. 'Can good people who are … desperate … also help the Fae take over?'

Pal nodded, stroking his chin. 'Aye. Desperation can lead humans to make unwise bargains, but no human ever prospers. Mark no doubt rules over them now. He will have lied and cheated to gain their trust. He will have made promises he won't keep. But less talk – we must hurry!'

* * *

When we reached the cairn, even from a distance, it looked … different somehow. Stones weren't stuck together in a neat tower any longer. It was demolished, as if a bomb had hit it. Less than half the size it had been … a thing of beauty, nearly completely destroyed.

Pal howled, and with a burst of energy bolted forward – raking his hands over the ground as if digging out a loved one. Stones were thrown all over the place, far away from where they should have been. Larger stones were scratched and chipped, no longer smooth but etched with swirls and criss-crosses.

Pal crumpled to his knees and, breathing raggedly, slammed both hands over his face. 'I have failed.' His voice was muffled. 'I have failed!'

He sounded so broken. Sometimes there were no

words; I put my hand on his arm and squeezed. I couldn't believe the destruction before us.

'We'll help you, Pal!' Nat, sobbing, threw himself on to Pal's back. 'There's nothing we can't do together. We're magic!'

'Your tricks are not real magic!' Pal tossed him aside. 'This is no game!' he roared.

We leaped back, stunned. Arlene put her hand over her mouth. She held out her arms and Nat ran to her; she hugged him close.

Silently, frozen, we watched Pal scour his hands over the loose scattered stones, sometimes lifting one, clutching it to his chest, wailing.

After a long while, he turned to us, his expression dull, his skin no longer shiny, but as if someone had ground a fistful of dust into his face.

'The cairn is enchanted. The doorway cannot be breached from inside, only opened from the outside. This means that a human from this realm, someone who knows magic and understands the power of these lands, has violated this sacred space.'

'Who would do such a thing?' asked Lloyd. 'Who'd dare come here to destroy this special place?'

I stepped forward, as did Arlene and then Nat too. We picked up large stones and cradled them. The stone I held had been warmed by the sun, and I felt as if I were cradling a delicate, injured bird. We held our beloved broken cairn in our arms and Arlene started humming quietly. The wind joined her, circling us. We listened to the waves break against the cliffs, as together we placed the stones back where they belonged. But they wouldn't stay. Whatever magic had connected them and held them together no longer worked, and they toppled back into piles, pieces of them chipping off as they tumbled.

'I know not what to do.' Pal stared at the stones plummeting to the ground. 'Alas, I have no magic. Not only that, but in this time and place, I have no steed, sword, or even much physical strength.'

The sky was gloomy and brooding, reflecting what we all felt inside: doom and uncertainty. Wind swirled around my neck, and I pulled my cardigan closer. It was hard to tell the difference between sea and sky with the mist rolling in.

'Your oath to protect won't be broken, will it, if you stop the Fae?' I asked Pal gently. 'We can help.'

He murmured, 'You are but children,' and wouldn't look at us.

'But we can be your allies,' I insisted. 'I can be your ally.'

'I need no allies,' Pal said, stiffening. 'I need *magic*. Merlin promised me magic. I swore an oath to guard the entrance to Fae Feld; to ensure no one came in or out. The doorway is open, and yet I cannot put these stones back together. No magic surges through my bones. I touch these sacred stones and I feel nothing. *Nothing!* They are simply stones and I – I am only a man.'

Pal had closed his eyes halfway through speaking. The four of us looked to him and we waited. What was there to say? I had no words to comfort him; none of us did. Lloyd knelt next to Pal. He picked up a large broken stone. 'Your quest isn't over,' he said. 'Tell us what we can do.'

'If I do not have magic, then there is no hope.'

'There's always hope!' Nat said insistently.

There had to be *something*.

'The only object which can help me is a grimoire.'

We stared at Pal blankly. 'A what?'

'A grimoire is a special book of spells and ancient

magic. Mortals cannot usually look upon it without becoming bewitched. Inside a grimoire lives secrets. It will tell us how to seal the doorway again.'

Pal looked into my eyes. As he did so, his eyes cleared. He drew himself up straight. Instead of the sapling he'd withered to, once again he was the mighty oak.

I said firmly, 'Just tell us who we're dealing with; how to beat them!'

We could do this.

Nat and Arlene had kept their distance but now they bounded over. Pal rested his hands lightly on their heads.

'You call your merry band the Roamers?'

Arlene nodded and Nat grinned. 'That's us.'

'You Roamers are kind and pure of heart. I know this to be true from the way you have protected and restored me. You have asked nothing of me and have given so much. Now, I need your help further. Understand – the Fae are cunning and ruthless. The Fae have powers beyond anything you've experienced before in your world. They can make you see and believe whatever they want. It's called *glamour*. If they wish to claim this land, then they will require a base – the heart of the town to begin their takeover. If Fae are here, a grimoire might well be too.'

Nat took Pal's hand. Pal glanced at their entwined fingers and smiled down at him.

'Now, you Roamers must return to Fablehouse before the church bells ring and the darkness comes. I am weary; sleep calls to my bones.'

'Will Merlin come and give you your magic now?' Nat asked hopefully.

Pal sighed. 'I hope so. The magic within me was supposed to be ignited upon any breach.'

'Think it was them village kids who opened the doorway?' Arlene asked.

Pal said, 'I do not know. But I must remain here now, at my post. I will guard the doorway and make sure no more Fae enter your world.'

'You not coming back with us?' asked Nat, his lips trembling.

Pal shook his head. 'My rightful place is here. I fear I ought not to have deserted my post at all. Perhaps Merlin has been already but found me wanting. He may still come to me, in a vision or dream. Then I shall repair the doorway.'

My voice quivering, I asked, 'But if the Fae are already here – what can we do?'

'Keep vigilant. It is *vital* to not let on that you recognise their deception. Changelings may look human, but they will not behave the same. Stay close to each other. You will need to look for a book. And whatever you see or hear, do not be swayed by anything which tempts you away from your quest. Stay true to yourselves. I will not leave my post again, come what may. I will defend your world with everything I have. No further Fae will pass through.'

I let Pal's words sink in. Staring into his face, lips set firm and jaw determined, I knew that he would do his best, but if the Fae looked like us and had magic too, then how would we ever know we were in danger? How many had already crossed over? This was worse than not knowing how to help Pal. This felt like fighting blindfolded, with our arms tied behind our backs.

Pal placed his hands on my and Lloyd's shoulders as he gave us all a solemn nod. 'Roamers. The future of Fablehouse, and the human realm, is in your hands now.'

Chapter Nine

All Change

B ack at Fablehouse, the four of us lounged listlessly in the battered armchairs in the common room as rain lashed against the bay windows. I felt helpless, and by the silence and others' expressions, I knew they felt the same.

My stomach knotted as I thought of Carole and Henry. How I'd seen them every morning, always smiling and chirpy; but now, even though they looked the same, they didn't act the same. Their eyes had no expression, no life, and there was a sly, sneaky energy that accompanied their mannerisms.

The Fae have powers beyond anything you've experienced

before in your world. They can make you see whatever they want. It's called glamour, *Pal had said. But what did this really mean? They could look like humans, so where were the real Carole and Henry now? Fae took people over? Where did they take them? If the Carole and Henry I'd seen at breakfast were changelings, who else was in danger and how could we stop this?*

Everyone at Fablehouse had already been abandoned. We were unwanted. Was that why the Fae had come here – did they think no one would notice? Were they targeting us because no one would miss us? How dare they!

'It's not fair!' I blurted out. The others looked at me, surprised. 'It's not fair what's happening and what Pal's been asked to do . . .' I struggled to get my words out. 'He's never even got to lead his own life! Watching an entrance to another world for hundreds of years – how is that a proper life?'

'It's not really, is it?' Lloyd said. He moved beside me and put his hand on my shoulder. 'I know, H.'

'And now us! Everything – we've just found each other, and now it's going to be taken away!'

I could barely even get out the words. I stared at

the rain streaming down the windows; inside I knew that my tears wanted to come out and do the same.

Lloyd leaned against the window, his nose pressed up to the glass. Nat and Arlene traced raindrops with their fingers, seeing which drop reached the bottom of the pane first, but Nat's appeared to be flickering and moving upwards.

I blinked. What if ... what if the strange things I'd seen lately, what if they were connected to the Fae? Like my reflection in the mirror?

I cleared my throat. 'We *have* to do something. If Carole and Henry are Fae, then ...' The words dried on my lips; I had no idea what we could do. I looked over to Lloyd, but he didn't move.

Arlene put her palm flat against the windowpane. 'What *can* we do?' she said quietly.

Nat sniffled. 'We need Pal.'

'Well, he's not here, is he?' I snapped, unable to keep my frustration in any longer. 'You heard him! It's up to us now. We have to be the ones to work out what's going on.'

Lloyd turned around, pressed his lips tightly together. He looked at me and nodded. 'We need to understand how bad it is here. First we need to work out who else might already have been changed. We don't know how many Fae are among us. Let's watch everyone carefully and note anything unusual. We'll report back to each other after supper?'

'That's not good enough!' I blurted. 'We can't just sit around taking notes!' I stood up, exasperated, and threw my hands in the air.

'We've got to protect the others – we could set traps!'

'H,' Lloyd said patiently. 'We don't even know how to catch or trap them. Plus, Pal said not to let them know we're on to them. I know it's hard, but the best thing is to try and act as normal as possible. Really. It's for the best.'

I chewed my lip, thinking hard. 'I read once that salt wards off evil spirits? Maybe it'd work on the Fae too? It can't harm to sprinkle some around, can it?'

Lloyd gave me a smile; he knew I had to do something. 'Maybe not.'

Nat sprang up and said, 'Maybe I can do some of my magic!'

'That's not *real* magic,' Arlene griped. But seeing

Nat's face fall, she added hastily, 'I mean, maybe a trick or two could be good for distraction, you might be right.'

Magic. I thought of Pal being denied his magic. I hoped Merlin would return and give it to him, but what if he didn't? It seemed obvious that Pal had been abandoned in this time and place. And what about the book he said he needed – a grimoire? Where would we find one of those?

The only books I knew of were the ones in Miss Isolde's office. All those boxes and books piled on her desk ... Wait! I had the Dead Arthur book, but there had been others. She'd found a bunch in the attic, hadn't she? That huge brown leather one with the fancy gold lock. Could that be the grimoire? How could we get to it ... ?

'Everyone will be back from church soon,' Lloyd said. 'So let's keep an eye out for anything strange, especially how Carole and Henry are behaving.'

Arlene nodded. 'OK, but now me and Nat have to help Miss Gloria lay the table.'

'Stay close to Davey,' I added. 'I didn't see him this morning, but maybe make sure that Carole and Henry leave him alone.' I didn't know how the Fae had got to them, but I didn't trust those changelings one bit. It seemed a good idea to keep the changed and non-changed away from each other – better to be safe than sorry.

'And where are you two going?' Nat asked.

'Got to keep up appearances. I'm on supper duty with Martha and Ruth, and Lloyd's with Leon on coop clear-out and egg collection.'

* * *

In the kitchen, Cook stood over the stove, stirring a pot of vegetable soup. Martha washed dishes while Ruth dried them. I grabbed an apron off the back of the door.

'Kitchen duty started ten minutes ago, Heather,' Cook admonished, peering at me. 'Here, chop these mushrooms, please.' She pointed at the worktop and chopping board laid out.

'Sorry, lost track of time,' I muttered, my cheeks flushing.

Martha and Ruth both gazed at me, giggling. I frowned at them, trying to see if they looked any

different to usual. *How would I know if they were Fae?*
Should I try to speak to them, or was it safer to avoid them?

With my back to the sink chopping the mush-rooms, I shivered. I knew I was being watched – could feel their eyes crawling all over me. Martha and Ruth were whispering, but I couldn't catch any actual words. Why was Cook being so quiet? She usually chattered away about the weather and village gossip, but now she just grunted to herself as she stirred the pot, making sure it didn't boil over. I liked Cook, even when she forced us to eat more boiled vegetables. I suddenly stopped chopping as a horrible thought pierced my mind: could the Fae change adults too?

I took the chopping board over to Cook. She scraped the mushrooms into the pot. Noticing the fruit bowl on the corner, I wrinkled my nose at the rotting oranges, bright with green fuzz, dripping juice on to the counter.

'Shall I throw those out?' I asked, pointing at them.

Cook paused her stirring and glanced at the bowl, horrified. 'We may not need rationing any more, young lady, but there's no place for needless waste!'

'But they're—'

'Very juicy?' Martha said, sneering and laughing.

What? I screwed my eyes tight shut and opened them again. But they were right – there was nothing wrong with the oranges now. No green, no fuzz. Was my mind playing tricks? Why was I seeing things that weren't there? Was this part of the 'glamour' Pal mentioned, or was I ... was I being taken over by the Fae? Was this how things started?

I still wasn't sure about Martha and Ruth. They weren't acting exactly how Carole and Henry had, but maybe different Fae acted differently too, like humans did? Or maybe they acted like the people they took over in some way? Oh, *why* hadn't we asked Pal more questions? This was hopeless!

Sneaking a glance at Martha, I shuddered. Was this the real Martha? She wasn't someone I knew well; I'd heard her tease the younger ones, so stayed away. If she was Fae now ... not only was she mean, but maybe dangerous too? What happened if the Fae knew that we were on to them? What would they do to us? I felt scared and unprepared and had no idea what I should do.

One thing was clear though: I needed to be careful, and not draw attention to myself. I couldn't tell Cook what I thought I'd seen, not without sounding like I'd been drinking from the same deep well of crazy they claimed my mother had.

Even if Cook *did* listen, I knew better than to trust a grown-up. 'Tell me if anything's wrong,' they always said, but then if you ever did, they'd tell you off, not believe you or, even worse, fail to understand at all. No, some thoughts were better kept inside, or only shared with people who would truly understand and really be on your side.

'Good work, girls!' Cook announced, taking off her apron and hanging it on the back of the door. 'You can go early.'

Martha and Ruth huddled together putting crockery away. I glanced at them, but they didn't turn to look at me. *Were* they changelings? I hadn't noticed any eerie green glow, and they'd not smiled enough for me to see their teeth. I'd tell the others that Martha and Ruth were safe for now. But what about the rest?

* * *

The corridors were deathly quiet. I glanced at the grandfather clock to check how long we had before supper, but the pendulum wasn't swinging – wasn't natural – a clock that didn't tick. It made me uneasy. I hurried back to the common room and pushed open the door, wrinkling my nose.

'What's that smell?' I asked. The common room stank of damp earth, mushrooms, moss. Pungent, like soil after it's been churned up and you've found worms under the ground.

Over at the windows, I fiddled with a catch.

'It's raining! Leave those windows be,' Miss Betty said. 'I can't smell anything.' She gave me an odd look and went back to darning the socks in her lap.

Glancing at the wireless on the sideboard, I frowned – there was a dreadful hissing coming from it.

'Shall I turn that off?' I asked Miss Betty.

She glared at me. 'And miss my programme? I think not. Now, you stop your fussing. Sit down there and be quiet, will ya?'

Miss Betty couldn't hear it.

I sat on a bench, trying to calm my breathing. Why was I the only one seeing things? What was wrong with me? What was wrong with *them*? I tapped my fingernails impatiently on the bench, wanting the others to get here.

I breathed through my mouth so I wouldn't smell anything, and watched Michael and Henry playing Snakes and Ladders on the carpet. Carole and Judy were in armchairs opposite me, both holding cloth dolls, bouncing them on their knees. Where was Jeremiah? He and Judy were usually inseparable. And Davey? I hadn't seen Davey!

'Heya, Judy.' I waved at Judy, calling out, trying to keep my voice light. 'Where's Jeremiah?'

Neither girl glanced at me, although the boys playing Snakes and Ladders looked up briefly. They both waved, but neither smiled and their waves were stiff. Prickles of cold shot along my neck and down my shoulders. Judy leaned over to Carole and whispered into her ear. She stared right at me. Then she grinned.

Her teeth were pointed!

I jumped up, pushing the bench back. Even across the room I could sense a strange energy, a shimmer of dark green mist hanging in the air above the girls.

I glanced at Miss Betty – she hadn't even looked up. I turned round sharply, almost bumping into Arlene and Lloyd, who were walking in. I grabbed at their sleeves and yanked them back into the corridor.

'I think – I don't know – but maybe they've all been turned by the Fae?'

'Really?' Arlene's brown eyes went wide and her lip wobbled.

'What makes you think that?' Lloyd asked.

'Just – no one seems quite like themselves.'

'Yeah.' Arlene twirled a lock of hair that had come loose round her finger. 'And when Jeremiah ran past us, I'm sure he looked ... sort of green round the edges?'

'That's what I saw!' I exclaimed, as my stomach dropped. A thought flew into my mind.

'Arlene ... was Miss Gloria acting odd?'

'No.' She wrinkled her nose. 'I don't think so, though whenever she spoke to us, she kept covering her mouth with her hand. Nat reckoned she'd been eating onions!'

'Leon was smashing eggs when I reached the coop.' Lloyd frowned. 'Definitely not behaving as he usually would. I mean, he's boisterous, but not ... destructive. Who's in the common room?'

'Carole, Judy, Henry and Michael. And where's Nat? You're supposed to stay together!' I urged.

'Nat's in the privy.' Arlene shrugged. 'What? I weren't going to follow him in there, was I?' She rolled her eyes.

'And Davey?' I asked, my voice rising in panic. I hadn't seen Davey since Miss Isolde had taken him off. And that was *yesterday*!

Arlene said slowly, 'I ... I haven't seen him.'

'So –' I counted on my fingers – 'that's five of us who might have already been turned? *Five!* That's nearly half. And no grown-ups have said or noticed anything. Think they're being turned too?'

'Pppft. Grown-ups always act strange,' Arlene huffed. 'How would we know?'

She had a point. I turned to Lloyd. 'Lloyd, what do you think?'

He thrust his hands into his pockets and started pacing. 'I think we need help.'

'From who?' I asked, exasperated. 'We're on our own with this!'

'Maybe not,' Lloyd said. 'Let's go and see Miss Isolde. If anyone can help, she can.'

We'd been told not to disturb Miss Isolde, but I thought of her books . . . What if she did have the one Pal needed? Even though we'd sworn no grown-ups before, maybe seeing Miss Isolde now wasn't such a bad idea.

Chapter Ten

The Head

Supper was quiet compared to the normal chatter. Davey, Miss Isolde, Miss Gloria and Leon didn't even come to the table and the others barely ate a thing. Us Roamers stuck together at one end of the table, discussing the best time to head to Miss Isolde's office.

As soon as Cook called in for table clearers and washer-uppers, we decided that was the moment.

The clock struck 6 p.m. The noise echoing through the deserted corridors startled us, after the clock had been still all day. Everything was topsy-turvy. We walked slowly away from the chimes, towards Miss Isolde's office, and the lights in sconces along the corridor flickered, the fringes fluttering. Suddenly a chill whipped round my neck and I spun around.

A small figure, in shadow, stood at the end of the corridor, right next to the clock.

'Davey?' I whispered, my heart pounding. I squinted and stepped towards him, but he darted away, off to one side.

'Where?' Nat asked, turning round to look at where I'd been staring.

'I ... I thought I saw him,' I muttered, now not certain I'd seen him at all. Each step we took, the air around us shivered colder, and then right in front of us, one of the framed paintings lining the corridors tilted, and then fell off the wall. I put my arm in front of Nat so that he didn't step in the broken glass.

'What's happening?' he asked, worried.

We stared at the smashed glass in front of us. Was someone, or something, trying to stop us reaching Miss Isolde's office?

'Come on,' I urged. 'Let's hurry up!'

The smell of damp grass and autumn leaves

became stronger the closer we got to her office door.

'Eww, look at those,' Arlene said, pointing at slimy snail trails all along the skirting boards.

It was as if the outside were making its way inside and taking over.

Why hadn't any grown-ups noticed anything? But then I was used to grown-ups not really noticing. They were always in such a rush that it was often unbelievable they even remembered we existed!

But Lloyd was right – Miss Isolde wasn't the same. The four of us reached Miss Isolde's door, but once there we just stared at each other, unsure of what to do.

'Knock then,' Nat said, indicating that I should do it.

'Why me?' I griped, my stomach knotting. 'Coming here was Lloyd's idea!'

Lloyd swallowed, his face drawn and anxious, so I said, 'All right, keep your hair on!' and raised my fist to knock twice, firmly.

'Enter!' Hearing her deep, warm voice, I confidently turned the brass doorknob and flung open the door. We'd come to the right place.

Miss Isolde was at her desk reading through papers. She looked up and smiled, but the smile was tight – frozen in place as if painted on. She leaned her elbows on the desk and put her fingers together in a pyramid. 'And to what do I owe this ... pleasure?'

She didn't look like seeing us was a pleasure.

We hadn't really decided on what to say, but somehow everything just tumbled out at once.

'We can't find Miss Gloria ...' Nat began. 'And there's a dead chicken and—'

Then Arlene chimed in. 'Judy and some of the others are acting funny. I don't think they're quite ... themselves.'

She could say that again.

I waited for Lloyd to add something, but he hung back, staring at the maps on the walls and the books lining the heavy shelves.

I willed Lloyd to look at me or to speak up – the adults always trusted and believed him – but he said nothing. Something wasn't right here; he sensed it, and then, in a rush, I did too.

'Is that all?' she asked, barely looking up from her papers.

That wasn't like Miss Isolde. I stepped forward, clearing my throat. 'Miss ... they're not being silly – Nat and Arlene. We need your help.'

'Help?' She threw her hands in the air. 'Yes, you certainly do – you can barely help yourselves!' Standing up, she glided around us and closed the door, leaning against it.

Blocking our exit.

She loomed over us, looking suddenly stretched somehow – thinner and much taller. All the hairs on my arms stood on end.

'Let's start with you!' She pointed at Nat. 'You, little Nat ... That's right, you are exactly like a gnat, a flea. Always hopping around. Getting into everything, irritating everyone with your tricks and constant questions. Why is that, little Nat? Afraid that if you stand still, no one will look at you, hmm? Is that it?'

Nat scrunched up his face, and his eyes swam with tears as Miss Isolde's razor-sharp words sliced him from the inside out. He moved to hide behind Arlene.

'People only tolerate you and *pretend* to believe in your stupid magic tricks because they're more entertaining than you could ever be! No one dares admit the cold and ugly truth. None of you are going anywhere. No one is taking you to their warm, cosy home. No one wants you. Do you still think your father will come one day? Oh, dear boy, how deluded could you possibly be?'

Why was she saying such awful things?

'Nat, I don't think she knows what she's saying!' I shouted, but Nat didn't seem to hear me. He was staring at Miss Isolde, his face slack and lips trembling.

'You're a *joke*,' Miss Isolde carried on. 'And not a very funny one at that. No one will ever take you seriously. Mind you – why should they?'

'Don't listen to her!' I put my hands over my ears and looked at Lloyd, but he looked almost frozen in place. Nat and Arlene gazed at her as if hypnotised.

'Miss, that's not fair!' Arlene cried bravely.

'*Fair?*' Miss Isolde said, moving into the middle of the room and towering over Arlene. She pointed her finger, eyes blazing. 'That's one thing you'll never be, isn't it, dear? *Fair!* The only person who cares about you is yourself!'

Miss Isolde mimicked a high mocking tone and held her skirts out, fanning them, miming as if she were twirling. '*Look at me, I'm Arlene! Look at me!*'

I watched her spin around, my eyes dazed as the colours swirled and ran together; everything flashing green and grey and brown.

Arlene wheezed, her eyes filling with tears and her shoulders heaving.

'Ignore her!' I screamed. Arlene's brimming eyes were fixed on Miss Isolde's mouth, but her lips glowed, shimmered lime-green, and as she sneered, I noticed her sharp teeth, as if they'd been filed into razor-like points.

'I think ... I ...' Lloyd croaked, and then sort of fell against the wall, as if all the stuffing had been knocked out of him.

'It's the Fae!' I shouted. 'They've got to her!'

Arlene shrank back into a corner of the room, turning her head away, sniffling. But Miss Isolde carried on with her cruel taunts, an endless parade of them.

'You will never be beautiful. Your wiry hair is a matted tangle, everything about you is chunky and clunky. You should never dance, you have the grace of an elephant! No matter how neat your plaits are, your kinks and coils will always burst free. Your eyes will never be as blue as cornflowers, your skin never peachy. No books or films exist with maidens or princesses who look like you! And you may squawk and warble, but no one will ever listen because you aren't worth listening to!'

I couldn't believe what I was hearing or seeing – my Roamers, crying and cowering from the vicious words spoken by someone who was supposed to care for them.

A feeling of anger that I hadn't had for ages bubbled up in my stomach, an inferno. Hot and fiery, it swelled and surged up my throat, gurgling behind my lips.

How dare she speak to my friends like this?

None of us needed to listen to this! If Miss Isolde couldn't help us – if the Fae had taken her – we just had to see if the book Pal needed was here and then get out!

Miss Isolde was nose to nose with Arlene by the door, so I strode over to her desk and pushed the papers aside. Now I was focused on a purpose, my anger simmered down to a low roil.

And there, underneath the papers, was the enormous brown book. The one with the lock. I leaned over, staring at it hard, feeling heat shimmer all around it.

Miss Isolde had her back to me, still berating Arlene. I placed my palm on top of the book. A light shone under my hand a little, like when you press a torch up against your skin. I felt the metal and twitched as it slowly began to heat up. I tried to slow my breathing as the lock became hot to the touch. The gold lock creaked and buckled, and as I snatched my hand away, the lock clicked, and the heavy cover flew open. As I glimpsed swirls and symbols across the pages, my head pounded.

What had just happened? This had to be the grimoire!

Perhaps Miss Isolde heard or sensed something because she suddenly whirled round. 'And you!' She wasn't focused on me or the desk though – she reached across the room to seize Lloyd by his collar. She dragged him into the centre of the room and lifted him clean off the ground. My mouth opened as I watched his feet dangle.

'*You.* No spine, no backbone. You'll do anything and everything to be liked. People-pleaser! We know your holier-than-thou attitude is fakery. You're wasting your time trying to convince everyone that you're perfect. Boys your age never get adopted. No one wants a stinky boy tearing up the place! Stinky boys become lazy, useless men! Shame you weren't born a hundred years ago, you might have proved useful – shoved up some chimneys! H*a!*'

Trying my best to blank out her words, I turned back to the book. There had to be something here we could use!

My eyes scanned the swirls and symbols on the pages, and even though I couldn't make sense of them, something inside whispered to me. I felt it, the sound of earth rustling beneath the cairn … a power reaching out. But it was pulling me away when – no, I had to stay here. I had to do something. I *had to*.

The Fae Miss Isolde was destroying my friends!

I faced her as she dropped Lloyd on the carpet and brushed off her hands. 'Do you imagine by saying, "Yes, miss, no, miss, three bags full, miss," that people will forget what you are?'

Her voice was a deep growl, like a caged beast. Her nostrils flared.

'And lastly, who do we have here? Ah yes. Heather.' Her voice was as soft as butter as she finally faced me. 'Heather, Heather, Heather,' she purred, as if my name were a chant.

'You always want the truth, don't you?' she said icily. 'Prize it, seek it out. Clinging to a belief that honesty *means* something. But people who insist on the truth are rarely ready to hear it – even if they claim they are. Well, I have some truths for you! You *are* too much. Loud. Opinionated. You laugh too loudly; feel too deeply. Your mother suffers the same affliction of intensity – it's abnormal, unseemly, to let such passion rage within you. People do not like such displays of longing. When you want too much and reveal all, it makes them uncomfortable. Hunger like yours can never be satiated.'

That stopped me in my tracks. Prickles, like sharp barbs, spread up and down my arms. As if she'd thrown a bucket of ice over me, my fury sizzled before melting away. And like a fire left cold in the grate, I felt cold, ashy, lifeless.

Then the cover slammed shut. The lock glowed and then died out. I gasped. *What had I done?*

Sadness lapped at my edges, the undertow luring me under, and before I could think, she said, 'Your mother was right.'

My mother?

'About what?'

'About you being unloveable. She claimed your temper would be the death of you. Said you ought to be hidden away. And look – here you are. Hidden. We can't even give you away. No one wants you!'

Suddenly I felt tired. Bone exhausted. I could lie down here happily, let the Fae take me ... wherever they wanted ... I was done fighting; done trying. There was no one to help us. I felt more alone than ever before.

No! This was what the Fae wanted me to think. But I wasn't alone, I had the Roamers, and I had to get them out of there somehow.

Taking deep breaths, I focused on Miss Isolde's mouth – her dark lipstick sticky. I examined every inch of her face, usually pale and soft and smiling, but now all I saw were eyelashes spiky as spiders' legs, thick red rouge like blood on her cheeks, and chalky powder dusting her forehead like ash.

What was I seeing? I could see through and beyond the Fae's glamour. I saw through the veil, into the truth – just like the rotten fruit. An image of Pal laughing, with orange juice dribbling down his chin, looking happy, popped into my mind. I gritted my teeth. Pal and my friends. I had to protect them!

This *wasn't* Miss Isolde, and I knew it. The others were enchanted though, couldn't take their eyes off her, believing and taking to heart her hurtful words. I knew adults said unkind and untrue things. Sometimes it was just their madness talking and not really them, but the adult here wasn't even . . . *human*.

Pal had said the Fae could make us see whatever they wanted us to see. And here we were being shown our deepest, darkest fears. The fears that gave us nightmares, which kept us smiling, even when we most felt like crying; the fears that kept us afraid to really show who we were.

We had to stay calm, so she wouldn't suspect that we knew she wasn't the real Miss Isolde. I wasn't sure how the Fae had got to her, or how any of the changelings had replaced the others, but I wasn't going to let that happen to any of the Roamers.

I was getting them out of there!

I said loudly, 'You're right, Miss Isolde. So wise.' I tried to hide my shaking voice. The others turned to me, puzzled, and I reached for them as I moved towards the door, pulling them close to me; trying my hardest to shield them. 'I *am* all those things you said.' Then, sweetly as I could, I said, 'We didn't mean to disturb you. We'd best get along.'

Lloyd finally seemed to come to his senses and grasped what I was trying to do. He moved quickly to the office door and held it open for us. I guided Nat and Arlene, both snivelling, past Miss Isolde, hoping she wouldn't make a grab for them. But she seemed to have lost interest in us now and turned back to her desk.

'Night, miss,' I said. 'Thank you for all your ... help.'

Chapter Eleven

The Truth

None of us spoke, but as we crept down the corridors I couldn't keep quiet any longer.

'You know she's Fae, right? She must be! She wasn't herself. She just said what she knew would hurt us the most!'

Lloyd nodded. 'I know, I guessed that, but still ...' His eyes dulled. The words Miss Isolde had said echoed through his mind again, I could tell.

'Listen,' I said. 'We can't let this distract us. Children and grown-ups are being taken over. We can't let them replace us!'

Arlene sighed. 'She was so ... mean,' she

breathed, her eyes wide. 'I just . . .'

They were all in shock, lifeless.

Nat had started crying again, his arm thrown over his eyes. We'd get nowhere if we let what she said poison our minds and hearts.

'Come on, Roamers! Really – you shouldn't listen to anything she said. It's all nonsense! Pal said the Fae were cruel and cunning, remember? But I think I found the book, the one Pal needs. It's right there on her office desk.'

'I've never had such horrible things said to me before,' Arlene murmured.

I kept wanting to say something, to offer comfort, but the words stuck in my throat. 'I know. But at least now we know what we're dealing with! Changelings. We ain't never gonna confuse them with the real people, are we? We need to focus on what we can do, how we can get rid of them. And if *that* Miss Isolde is a changeling, then what happened to our real one? Where is she? We have to find her and the others!'

'You're right.' Lloyd yawned. 'But I can barely keep my eyes open. We need to sleep.'

'I'm tired too,' Arlene said.

Tired? I could tell they were still smarting from Miss Isolde's words; but me? I was wide awake.

Lloyd ruffled Nat's hair gently. 'Come on, sleepy-head!'

'I'm having my bubble bath first,' Nat said. 'No one is stopping me doing that!'

'Night,' I replied, watching them head for the staircase.

'Coming, Heather?' Arlene asked, holding out her hand. I shook my head. I needed to be by myself for a bit. 'I'll be up in a little while,' I replied, turning on my heel and heading towards the common room.

*   *   *

It wasn't even 7 p.m. yet. From the floors above me, I heard scampering footsteps and low murmurs, but I hadn't seen a soul. It wasn't like Fablehouse to be this quiet, ever. I pushed open the common-room door cautiously. Suddenly being on my own didn't seem like a very good idea – like always, I'd just steamed ahead, not thinking things through. But the room looked empty. The shutters hadn't been closed yet and the sky was darkening, but still light. It was that enchanting dusky time when pinky-purple clouds mingle with the darkening shadows.

Before I reached for the light, there was a clinking noise. I squinted into the gloom and there, right at the back of the room, wedged between a toy chest and a threadbare armchair, was Davey. He had his head down low, his cap off to one side. He was playing marbles. *Clink.*

'Davey!' I exclaimed, joy seizing my heart as I rushed forward to him. But he didn't turn around, didn't lift his head to look at me. There was a swallow, so loud in the silence of that room, and then a raspy croak as he opened his lips to speak, repeating, 'Davey – yaas.'

I stopped, only inches from him now, my breathing shallow. I knew immediately what had happened. *Davey was Fae.*

'Want me to play?' I said, trying to smile, trying to act normal even though my heart had snapped in two.

He lifted his head then, and his eyes were flecked with black. Clouds crashed through my mind as I realised that Davey was gone. *Oh, Davey!* What had the Fae done to him? I bit down on my tears. Where was he? How would I ever find him again?

'Yaas,' he lisped, nodding. 'Play.'

I knelt next to him and with shaking hands reached for a marble from a drawstring bag next to his knee. I rolled it and we both stared as it rolled across the floor. Davey snatched up a handful from the bag and flung them at my marble.

'Davey win!' he screeched, laughing, as they clattered against the walls.

'Well done,' I said, every part of me trembling with fear and panic. It felt like a wild animal next to me, one which might bite as soon as let me pet it.

I stood and brushed myself down. 'Bedtime for me.'

His hand shot out and cold bony fingers gripped my forearm. I held my breath as his sharp nails caught against my skin. 'Story?' he hissed.

I gulped, tried again to show a sincere smile. 'Maybe tomorrow?'

I turned abruptly and left the room, grimacing as I heard him cackling and muttering to himself. 'Maybe tomorrow... bedtime for me. Bedtime.'

Each step I took up the stairs to my room felt like I was climbing a mountain. My skin felt clammy.

Where was my Davey? I could hardly breathe as I crawled into bed ... couldn't stop picturing those black sparks in his eyes, his unchanging face like stone – no smile, no light that usually swam around Davey wherever he went.

*　*　*

Arlene whimpered long into the night, and I couldn't sleep. I kept seeing Davey as not-Davey. When Arlene's sobs finally dissolved into shuddering breaths and then snuffles, I hoped sleep might come for me too, but I couldn't forget Davey and the awful things Miss Isolde had said.

I saw images of my mum ... I imagined that the Fae had come for her. Every time she came near me, she'd start hissing and baring her teeth, revealing a furred green tongue.

I tossed and turned. I knew we had to fight this and yet I wasn't sure how we could. And I was tired ... I was always fighting, it seemed. Fighting to be heard, for what I thought was right – I'd finally got to a real place I could enjoy, with friends and a headmistress who I trusted, and now ... all of it was about to be taken away from me. I swallowed, my throat aching. My heart aching. A tear ran down my cheek and I dashed it away. I wasn't a crier; crying never did any good. No one ever came.

Maybe it just wasn't meant to be. Maybe I was never supposed to be happy; maybe people like me didn't deserve good things.

It was dark and I was alone. I thought of Mum locked away; how she'd only been young when I came along ... and now she wasn't allowed to do what she wanted either. Like Pal almost, forced into a life she didn't choose. And the more I thought of her, the more I thought of all the children abandoned here and how unfair that was. What had we ever done? We didn't ask to be born, but here we were, trying to make the best of things and have a good life, and now ...

I remembered listening to *Listen with Mother* on the wireless together; how she always smelt warm, of milk and Farley's rusks. How she would gaze at me with something like wonder. It wasn't true what Miss Isolde said – she *did* love me once! I know she did, I felt it. But her parents, over the years, wore her down, always speaking of shame and disgust, saying she'd disgraced them by having me. Refusing to be out with me in public. And I think . . . I think that's what broke her, in the end. Everyone else's judgement and disapproval.

When I was five, Mum was bundled, kicking and biting, into a big black car, and stared at me, helpless, from the back windscreen. She clawed at the seats and watched her father lift me up as if I were nothing. I screamed and clawed at him, but he held me tight, stopping me from running after her, my skirts flying as my fingers scrabbled in the dirt for my fluffy toy rabbit I'd tried to push into Mum's hands before they grabbed her. It wasn't her choice to leave me. Maybe she hadn't even wanted to. When she said mean things, like what Miss Isolde had said, maybe that had been her madness talking and not her.

Maybe I could forgive her . . .

And then I *was* bawling. I couldn't help it. Tears ran down my cheeks and into my bedsheets and across my pillow, soaking it. I turned my face into the pillow and sobbed and sobbed, trying to make sure I didn't wake Arlene. I cried so hard it was as if I'd been turned inside out, wrung dry. Eventually I wiped my eyes and sniffed. I should try and sleep. Then thoughts of my mother faded and instead those images morphed into the changing faces of the Fablehouse children, now with spiteful eyes and sharp teeth, their skin a ghostly, sickly green. What could we do to stop the changelings? Nothing! We couldn't do anything! They wouldn't leave us alone.

If they could take little Davey – innocent Davey who wouldn't hurt a fly – and Miss Isolde – a grown-up who was strong and sure of herself – then what chance did we stand? *None.*

Through the gap in our bedroom curtains, I saw it was still dark outside. An owl cooed in the distance. Lying in bed I decided I wasn't going to stay any longer. I refused to watch my friends being taken over and seeing Fablehouse be destroyed. If I couldn't help, if I couldn't stop this – then … I could just leave. I *didn't have to be here!*

This part of my life was coming to an end – the good times always did – and it was obviously time to move on. Time to get away and start over – I'd done it before. I could do it again.

Decision made, my shoulders relaxed.

I hurriedly stuffed a spare pinafore into a cloth bag, trying not to disturb Arlene, or remember how she'd often slip her hand into mine, changing song lyrics by adding in my name, the way Lloyd backed me up any time I was unsure, or the way Nat laughed till he cried at my jokes.

They'd be fine without me. Better off, probably.

I knew how to run – how not to look back. This was the Heather of old, the Heather who never really left me; the Heather who had my back and protected me at all costs. Maybe the Heather who always ran *was* the real Heather, and the Roamer Heather was as much a fake and phoney as them changelings. Maybe this whole time, the only person I'd been fooling had been myself.

Mum had slipped a crown into my hand before she was taken away. I always kept it in my boot in case I needed it. That would be enough for food and bus fare – enough to get me far away from here.

I crept down the stairs, careful to avoid the fifth one, which was extra creaky. The place was deathly quiet. Then I was out the front door and away.

* * *

The inky sky was clear and cloudless with sparkling stars beginning to make themselves known.

A steady calm settled over me as I headed through the dark, winding lanes towards the village. Trees loomed, casting strange shadows everywhere I turned, but I wasn't afraid. I'd get a bus to somewhere I could lie low, and then figure out my next move. Now the sky was lightening, and the air crisped around my shoulders. A few cars, and boys on bicycles, passed me on their way to work as the world woke up. Big prams were parked outside houses. I peered into one. Empty. *Strange.*

As I approached the bus stop, orange lights winked at me in the distance. *Oh no* – I'd just missed one! I peered at the faded timetable – not another bus for two hours. I leaned against the bus stop, staring along the quiet street – could I cadge a lift if I put my thumb out? Unlikely. They'd probably haul me back to Fablehouse; it was obvious where I'd run from.

I trotted across the road to look in the sweet-shop window. I pressed my nose up against the glass, looked at the glass jars behind the high wooden counter: penny chews, sherbet lemons, fruit pastilles. Movement out of the corner of my eye. I turned to see two children walking towards me, something about them that I recognised – their walk! It was the boy and girl who'd called me names the other day – who'd reported me, trying to get Miss Isolde and Fablehouse into trouble. What were they doing here? At this time?

There wasn't anywhere to run and hide. Anyway, why should I hide? They were the ones who started it. They should be the ones running! *Let them just . . . try it!* I clenched my hands into fists – if they wanted to start something, I'd be ready.

We were close enough to see each other clearly now. I stared right into those same eyes I'd seen before and . . . nothing. *Nothing.* They both stared ahead, barely registering me. Not even blinking. Surely they remembered me? I mean, how often did a 'hellion with wild curls', as Miss Isolde put it, hit them?

But they looked somehow . . . different. Their pale skin had a hint of green, their eyes blank and glassy. When the girl smiled in my direction, her teeth were pointy and razor-sharp. They passed me by. My heart pounded. *Changelings!* Even in the village. That meant the Fae's power *was* spreading – it wasn't only Fablehouse in danger.

I stared after the boy and girl as they moved silently through the early morning streets, footsteps barely touching the ground. A milkman on his rounds stopped his float and got out to deliver two pints to the cottage opposite the bus stop. As he pushed open the cottage gate, the children hopped on to the back of his float and started throwing milk bottles into the road.

Smash! Glass splintered everywhere.

Crash! Rivers of milk streamed along the road.

Their laughter was high-pitched and piercing.

'Oi!'

The milkman ran to his float and tried grabbing one of them, but the girl gripped him by the shoulders and threw him off. They both ran off laughing down the street.

Shaking, I slumped against the bus stop, turning my back on them so I didn't have to see any more. How could I run away now? What was the point – if

Fae were in the village, who knew how long it'd be before they reached the next village or town?

Scuffing my shoes along the ground, I thought about the children in Fablehouse waking up and going to breakfast ... Lloyd, Nat and Arlene might be the only ones not replaced now. Which put them in even more danger.

I couldn't leave my best friends to *this* – whatever this was. Wherever I ran to, the Fae would catch up with me, with all of us. There was no hiding, or pretending this wasn't happening. It *was* happening. It had happened. Fae folk were taking over and pushing us out. What choice did I have but to help my friends fight? They *were* my family, weren't they? And family didn't abandon each other when things got tough. Even if my mother *had* abandoned me ... I wasn't her. I could make my own decisions – different ones. How would things ever change unless I tried a different path?

I could only help if I stayed.

Running never solved anything, not really. I remembered the times I'd run away before. Aged seven and nine, I'd filled my pockets with food, crawled out of windows in the dead of night, and wandered the countryside with my hat pulled down low, fearful of every sound and glance. The exhilaration always settled to a dull ache when I realised that I'd have to go back. The cold truth always wormed its way into my mind and my heart, telling me what I always knew: *there is nowhere to run to.*

You never get far trying to outrun yourself.

Miss Isolde had opened Fablehouse. And when no one else wanted us, she'd given us food, care and attention – trying to make the world a better place. I saw her read to Davey and gather herbs from the garden; she was patient and kind. Now she needed our help; we had to find the real her and bring her back. Who knew what danger she was in?

I had to go back and stand up for those who couldn't stand up for themselves. I wasn't alone any more, and there was no use pretending that I was. I'd go back to Fablehouse, get the Roamers, get the book and take it to the cairn. We'd get rid of these Fae once and for all.

* * *

The birds were loud in the early morning. I nudged open the back door next to the kitchen and crept my way down the corridors. Miss Isolde never locked her office. She always claimed this place was our home and as such there was no place that was off limits.

I turned the office door handle. And there, right in the centre of her desk, as if it were waiting for me, was the grimoire. I snuck across the room and laid my hands on it – felt nothing. No warmth, no glow. Why had it opened before? I thought perhaps it had opened for me because I could see through the Fae glamour, but maybe not. There wasn't time to think about that now. Every moment I spent here, away from the others, could be dangerous. I had to get back to them and we had to stick together. I stuffed the book under my pinafore. It weighed a ton! I hoped Pal could decipher whatever magic was between these pages.

I backed out of Miss Isolde's office and pulled the door closed. As I turned round, I was greeted by a chorus of loud exclamations.

'There she is!' Nat cried out.

'Where have you been?!' Lloyd demanded, as Arlene fretted around me. 'We looked everywhere for you.'

'Everywhere!' She pouted.

Nat stared at me, unsmiling. 'Arlene said you weren't in bed ...' He frowned. 'That your clothes and bag had gone! You *left* us ...'

Heat blazed into my cheeks. I couldn't believe that I'd considered leaving them and that they'd been worrying about me. 'Just for a bit. Went for a nice long walk, you know. Clear my head,' I mumbled, but I couldn't meet their eyes.

Nat said, 'Can I have a hug?'

'A what?'

'A hug?' He threw his arms round my waist and pulled me close. His arms tightened and I couldn't move. Was I supposed to squeeze him back? I felt the curve of his fluffy hair under my hand, his head nestled into my belly. I gently squeezed back.

'It's OK,' I said, patting his back. Not because I thought it would be, just because it seemed like the right thing to tell him.

'You deserted us!' Arlene cried indignantly. 'Just like everyone else! Were you even gonna come back?'

Her words may have been spiky, but dried tears streaked her cheeks.

I sighed and moved to put my arm around her

shoulder. 'I *was* considering not coming back,' I admitted, clearing my throat. 'But then, you know, I thought about how much I'd miss you and your singing. Every time you sing it's so sweet and can't help but make me think beautiful thoughts. And you, Nat, because you really *are* magic, the way you always see the good in things, seeing potential everywhere.'

I paused, and Lloyd and I locked glances and my eyes rushed with tears to see my friend's face.

'And you, Lloyd, always so straight and true. Making sure we never take a wrong turn . . .' My voice dipped.

I'd miss all of you, your very essence.

Lloyd nodded, just once. That small movement of his head was everything. He knew exactly what had been going through my mind. The nod was his acceptance that I was welcome back, that he forgave me . . . and that he understood.

I wasn't alone.

'A walk can be useful for clearing the head,' he said, staring at me keenly. 'Anything come to you?'

'Yes,' I said, smiling at him. 'I've got the grimoire.'

Chapter Twelve

Grimoire

Although everyone was keen to give the book to Pal as quickly as possible, I couldn't stop yawning. We agreed that I'd go to bed and get a few hours' sleep while they covered for my absence during breakfast, and then, as soon as we could, we'd make our way to Pal and the cairn. We knew we were supposed to be in lessons, but what would be the point? Nat wondered if we should rush to the cairn immediately, but Lloyd said how that might draw attention to us and that it was sensible to wait for a more natural time to leave, so as not to arouse suspicion.

It seemed pretty certain that everyone now apart from us had been changed. The atmosphere in the whole house felt thick and charged. No one bothered to clear the dishes after breakfast and the bins in the common room were overflowing. We couldn't wait to get outside, to get away. But once we were stood on the lawn, it was as if the world was paused, waiting for whatever happened next. The curtains of Miss Isolde's office twitched, and Arlene said, 'Can we go now?'

I cradled the grimoire to my chest, and we set off.

* * *

The weather was strange too, as if a cloud had been thrown over the world. We could barely see five yards in front of our faces.

We decided to walk, and the mist followed us, rolling across the hills and threading itself through the trees. The wind whipped around us, teasing us almost, gusts coming from nowhere. I clutched the grimoire tighter. It was heavy though, so Lloyd and I took it in turns to carry it. I hoped Pal knew how to open the book and understood the symbols.

Cresting the hill, and seeing the cairn, a feeling of

hope skipped in my chest. I reached for Lloyd's hand, pulling him along, speeding up.

'Wait for us!' Nat yelled behind us.

But we couldn't wait, we just weren't able to. The cairn pulled us towards it. We ran across the moorland and the flowers and grass tangled us up underfoot. Seeing the stones, my heart ached. I gingerly approached the cairn first, ahead of everyone else. It felt very different around here now. The air had been churned up, full now of agitation and fear. No birds settled anywhere near here. A ring of black toadstools and mushrooms had sprung up around the stones and their gills moved back and forth. I felt as if I'd let the stones down somehow.

'I'm sorry,' I breathed, to the land, to the sky.

Pal was slumped over to one side, against the lower stones of the cairn, his eyes closed. I gently set the book down beside him and let my gaze move slowly over his face.

Did my own father look like this? I had no idea if he was even still alive. The last time I'd seen my mother, she described how handsome he was, how hard he fought 'those evil Nazis' ... I remembered how misty her eyes became, how faintly her voice dipped, as she described his starched, smart uniform and told stories of him flying planes through the sky . . . But those thoughts had no place here.

'Pal!' Nat rushed forward to sit next to him.

Pal shifted, sweat beading across his forehead. Arlene and Nat sat at his feet. He stretched and took us in, smiling gravely as he rubbed a hand wearily across his face.

'My Roamers,' he said. 'What news have you of the Fae?'

Our words tumbled over each other, rushing to come out.

'We went to see Miss Isolde—'

'We thought she might help—'

'But she was really mean!'

I put my hand on Nat's arm. 'It was clear that she wasn't herself,' I added. 'We think the Fae have got to her.'

'It's not good,' added Arlene. 'The Fae are *definitely* in Fablehouse.'

'And the village,' I added, coughing softly.

'The village?' Pal looked between us, frowning. 'No! Already?'

'But we've brought something that might help,' I said. 'This is the book that was on Miss Isolde's desk. She showed me this and the Arthur one at the same time. When I touched it yesterday, in her office, it sort of grew hot and flew open – I don't know why. But it hasn't opened again.'

Pal lifted the book on to his lap. He gazed at it with a mixture of awe and fear. 'This is indeed the grimoire.' His fingers traced around the lock. Laying his hands flat on top, he closed his eyes. 'There are many different versions of this sacred book. This one . . .' His gravelly voice slowed down. 'We must be careful; this book contains great power.'

Nat's mouth hung open, his eyes wide. 'What happens? Do things fly out of it?'

Pal shook his head. 'No. But the book makes promises it cannot keep. A grimoire is a trickster, an agent of chaos. Those who believe it turn stupid; people can regret ever setting eyes on the pages. But by then, it is too late.'

'Fancy!' Arlene's eyes widened. 'How could a book do all that?'

I cleared my throat. 'I did feel something when it opened, just briefly.'

Pal leaned forward, peering at me keenly. 'What did you feel? Do you know why it opened for you?'

I shrugged. 'I don't know ... Miss Isolde was – like the others said – being awful. I got so angry! It was as if I was going to explode! Then when I touched the book, the lock clicked and flew open.'

Pal nodded, deep in thought.

'Magic lives and breathes. This book is a sentient entity. I have heard that it feeds off strong emotions: anger, jealousy, fear, passion. But human eyes should not look upon it, for once it has taken your wits ... Only a sorcerer should be able to wield it.'

'You keep mentioning your magic,' Lloyd said, searching Pal's face hopefully. 'Did Merlin come to you?'

Pal's eyes dulled. 'No.' He stood up, gazing across the moorland. He brushed himself down. 'No one came to me.'

We fell to silence for a moment then. I knew we were all thinking of, remembering, a time when we had waited ... waited for those who would not come, to visit, or to take us home.

Arlene shifted over to sit next to me. She reached

for my hand and then Nat's. 'Can you use the book without magic?' she asked softly.

Pal turned back to us. He rubbed his chin. 'Perhaps.'

If *we could use it without magic* ... I rested my fingers on the gold lock. 'It's worked before?'

'But it can mesmerise you if you aren't careful,' Pal added gravely.

I said, 'What happens if *you* fall under its spell?'

Lloyd nodded. 'We won't be strong enough to stop you.'

'Could one of us open it?' Nat said. 'Then you can protect us if anything happens.'

Pal looked thoughtful. 'If Heather's energy opened the book before, if she can focus and direct her anger, then she *may* be able to resist any temptations or promises offered.'

'I could try,' I said. I dragged the book over.

Arlene smiled. 'You can do this,' she said kindly.

I looked to Pal and put my hands on top of the worn cover. 'What do I do now?' I let my fingers linger on the lock.

'The book draws energy from you. Hold questions

in your mind that you want answered. Focus as if your life depends on it. Remember your feelings from last night. But be on your guard; the book may try to trick you.'

Miss Isolde's words came back to me. *No spine, no backbone. Unloveable. Abomination. Unwanted. None of you are going anywhere. No one is bringing you to their warm, cosy home. No one wants you.*

Tears prickled my eyes. I closed them and my breathing slowed. Resting my hands on top of the book, I tried to remember the pages I'd seen when it had flown open before. But only Miss Isolde's words kept replaying in my mind, making me sad, empty and feeling small. And then I remembered what she'd said to Arlene and Lloyd and Nat – little Nat who wouldn't hurt a soul – and the anger came again. A glowing tight ball of wriggling, chomping fury unfurled inside me, heavy like a cannonball, and the raging pounding of my heart and my arms flared, heat coursing down my arms into my palms and – that was it. The metal lock under my palm burned bright. Jerking back, my hand came away as the lock squealed, bent, and the cover flew open.

Something moved, squirmed almost, underneath the brown leather, ink and inscriptions. Staring at lines and squiggles, symbols danced, spinning into patterns which made my eyes sore. I tried to keep my finger following along the lines.

The air grew silent and still, and though I tried to lift my head to smile at Nat and Arlene and Lloyd, the pages kept yanking my attention.

My head felt trapped in a grip too fierce to look away from. I gritted my teeth. Tried to keep saying in my mind, so I couldn't be distracted: *How do we save Fablehouse and my friends?*

'Heather.' Pal's voice was gentle. 'You are trying too hard. Faith is not found by effort and will. You will not find answers by controlling, only by letting go. Magic is a lightness of touch. Breathe deeply. Imagine your feet anchored to the ground. Feel your connection with the earth, the roots of the trees, all connected underground, communicating for miles, for centuries. Focus on feeling protected. Keep in mind the calm of this cairn. The land will hold you – *let it.*'

I waited for the book to speak to me. I tried to steady my mind, to relax by breathing slowly and evenly.

Friends? The word echoed around me, stinging me from one ear and then the other. *Do you not want a family?* Images flew thick and fast into my mind's eye, but they all seemed tinged with green, and no one looked quite how I remembered.

A family to call your own . . . We can give you a family . . . You can be happy . . . We can give you that. A family of your own. Wouldn't you like that? Parents who love you, who want you.

I tensed my stomach and gritted my teeth too. This must have been like when the madness came for Mum, made her believe that I was sent to ruin and shame her, but it wasn't true.

Could I resist?

Pal's voice came through to me, sounding strained and faint, as if he were very far away.

'What are they offering? Resist the dark magic. With your fire and integrity – hold still and the book may yield more. Become one with the pages, the paper, the leather, the ink. Do not feel alarmed. Hold us in your mind and allow us in – we will be able to hear the book speak to you.'

He was right. I felt as if I were being drawn,

pulled forward, my hands tight against the book, and I could barely breathe, like being sucked into a whirlpool. I couldn't move. Nervous, I rubbed my hands together and then laid both palms across the centre of the book. Heat crackled through my hands and prickled my fingertips. Goosebumps shivered up and down my arms and a freshness settled around me, as if someone had thrown a cold blanket around my shoulders.

I stroked the symbols, which warmed under my touch. The pages shimmered, flickers of heat waves rose from the pages, almost pulling my other hand back down on to the fragile pages.

You think you can challenge me? What makes you think you are enough?

Suddenly the ground under me began to shake. Leaves tore themselves from trees and flew around the cairn. The toadstools and mushrooms snapped and broke apart; frost formed and cracked across the stones, and my teeth chattered together as if it were the middle of winter.

Your fury may be fire, but ours is ice and will quench yours . . .

The book was speaking to me in my mind. The others heard it too; I saw their mouths moving and reacting, but I only heard the grimoire. I squeezed my eyes shut and said, out loud and firmly, 'I will not bargain!' before opening my eyes again.

You want answers.

'I do not want anything else you offer. I only want my friends. How can we get them back?'

I saw Pal and Nat and Arlene and Lloyd, but it was as if they were trapped behind a thin gauze veil, and I couldn't touch them. But I saw them watching me; Pal had his hand on top of mine.

The Fae have taken the humans into their realm. While they permeate the human world, your friends are at the mercy of their leader. There is only one way to get them back. Fae Feld awaits the brave and true.

'How can we stop them?' I croaked.

The Fae have a mighty leader, a warrior called the Champion. He shows no mercy and desires power above all else. But rid Fae Feld of the Champion, and you may stop the Fae swarming the earth. The Fae are under his control because he has promised them riches. Their greed makes them blind to his manipulations!

'Pal!' I turned to him, tears already on my cheeks. 'We need to go to Fae Feld!'

'But . . .' Pal stared at us, his voice full of bad news. 'The Fae realm is only for Fae. Humans are not permitted. If humans stay too long, then . . .'

'Then?' Nat badgered.

Pal lowered his head, staring at the ground. 'If humans stay too long in Fae Feld, they won't ever be able to leave.'

The Fae won't give the humans up. There will be no bargaining. You will have to defeat the Champion; show the Fae it is you who are superior.

I banged my fists on the book, hard. *And how could we do that?*

'There must still be time!' Arlene exclaimed.

Pal said, 'Hold me in your mind and ask the book where my magic is. Perhaps an answer will emerge.'

Break the spell on Pal, I thought, over and over, until the words felt like solid objects soaring above me.

Nothing.

I listened to my own steady rising and falling breaths. I felt Pal's warm hand on mine. *Break the spell on Pal. Give Pal his powers back,* I chanted over and over in my head.

No spell has been cast.

'Are you sure?'

He whipped his hand off mine and stood. I knew he'd heard the grimoire speak.

'Nonsense!' he tutted, lips pursed. 'The book weaves untruths.'

The one worthy of battle against the mighty warrior is the Chosen; this is what has been foretold through the sands of time. Only the Chosen will triumph.

'The Chosen?' I asked aloud.

Chosen have unseen powers which guide their path. Is there a Chosen among you?

Opening my eyes was tricky; it was as if they'd been glued together. I wrenched my hand off the book, my palm surging with warmth, and we all watched the lock flare white-hot before locking with a snap. It took me a few moments to focus on the others gazing at me.

'H?' Lloyd said, biting the inside of his cheek. He touched my shoulder. 'Are you OK?'

'You were scrunching up your face something

awful!' Arlene said. 'You couldn't hear us, we kept asking you things.'

'Your teeth were chattering so loud I thought they were gonna break!' Nat exclaimed.

I leaned back, exhausted. It was as if I'd been running, trying to escape something much faster than myself.

Lloyd's fists were clenched as he looked into my face for answers. 'You were doing a load of muttering.'

'What now?' I asked, searching Pal's features for an answer. 'Are *you* the Chosen?'

Pal shook his head. 'I am not. I am a knight, the protector and guardian of the cairn.'

Nat kicked the base of the cairn sulkily.

'What can we do, Pal?' Lloyd asked.

'You're the boss!' said Nat, still wanting to believe Pal could change things and help us, though I knew better now.

Pal sighed. He slumped and put his hand to his forehead. Any energy and fire he'd carried within him before had all but vanished.

'I am at a loss,' he said sadly. 'The humans need to be rescued from Fae Feld for the changelings to disappear.' Pal stared at us. 'But with no magic, what use will I be?'

'You're *our* Pal,' Nat said simply. 'Our friend.'

I wished he believed in himself enough so that his powers would return, but there he was, looking utterly defeated. Just a tired man, ancient and sad, in baggy carpenter overalls. But he wasn't just that, was he? He was so much more.

'Pal,' I said firmly. 'You're still a knight. The knight who defeated the Questing Beast! You'll always be a knight.'

I smiled at him, searching his face, but his head was down and his eyes fixed on the broken stones littering the ruined ground.

'Sometimes...' Arlene began. 'Oh, never mind.'

'What?' I asked. 'Go on.'

She winced and shook her head. 'Well, I was going to say ... sometimes when you feel bad, you have to sort of *pretend* to feel better, and then you *do* feel better.'

Pal scratched his head, looking confused. 'What do you mean?'

'If you tell yourself nice things, after a while,

you can start to believe them. Like in *Cinderella* – that song – "A Dream Is a Wish Your Heart Makes".' She started humming. 'You just have to keep wishing and dreaming for the things you want to be true.'

I loved Arlene's hopefulness, but making wishes and singing wouldn't help us here. We were running out of time and needed everyone safe and back at Fablehouse.

'Pal, if you don't have any actual magic, there isn't anyone else who can help us. We'll have to rescue them on our own,' I said, determined.

'We're not on our own, are we?' Lloyd looked at me. 'We have each other.'

'How can we rescue anyone?' Nat looked like he was about to cry. 'And what if we can't escape!'

'Pal said it's not for humans!' Arlene wailed.

Lloyd's eyes glistened, reflecting the wisdom of the trees. 'At least we'll be together,' he said, pressing his lips together. 'Anyway. H is right. We have to try.'

Arlene stood up. 'I suppose. We can't just sit around and do nothing, waiting for someone else to help!'

Looking round at the Roamers, I knew we had to

venture into Fae Feld to try and rescue our friends. We didn't have a choice; they were our family.

Pal cleared his throat. 'Roamers, are you certain?'

We all nodded.

I cleared my throat and put my hands on the book. Loudly I said, 'We choose each other as family, and we will fight to keep our home safe.'

'Spoken like true warriors.' Pal smiled at us, tears sparkling in his eyes. 'This will not be easy. But I will teach you.' He opened his arms and beckoned us in for a hug.

Chapter Thirteen

Warriors

'We should go to the lake,' Pal said.

'Why?' I asked. 'What's there?'

'When we were there before, that was when my memories returned. The Fae Feld – it is *as above, so below*.'

'What does that mean?' Nat said.

'Fae Feld is a mirror image of this world. It will have a lake, as we do here. Water is a very powerful element, and lakes hold concentrated magic; sometimes objects, often people. I do not think it a coincidence that my memory returned while we were next to water. Since the doorway has already been breached, and the balance of what is and what will be is disturbed, now in *this* realm our lake may have someone who can assist us. Heather, you already know the tale of the Lady of the Lake.'

I nodded. 'She gave Arthur his sword. It was said to be invincible.'

'But won't more Fae cross over if you leave your post?' Lloyd asked, looking worried.

Pal pressed his lips together. 'It *is* risky, but the biggest danger is at night. It is under cover of darkness when the veil between worlds is at its thinnest, but dusk is not yet upon us and if we go now, and quickly, we risk less.'

Pal hefted the grimoire under his arm and said, 'We cannot dally. Come!'

*　*　*

The lake was still and quiet. Reeds bristled around the edges. We stood behind Pal, eagerly wondering what he was going to do and what we would see. At the water's edge he knelt down. He put his fingers in the water and ripples lapped over his knuckles. A dragonfly with iridescent wings flittered past, stopping on the reeds nearest us. Pal began moving his fingers back and forth in the water, murmuring under his breath. It sounded like an ancient language, or a prayer.

Silence, stillness. The wind stirred through the trees. Nat and Arlene huddled together, and Lloyd and I watched Pal carefully, both of us thinking the same thing: was anyone here and what help might they give us?

I went and knelt down next to Pal. Being next to him, I saw how pained he looked.

'Do you think your magic will ever come?' I asked him.

He stopped for a moment, tilted his head to one side and listened to the birds chirping.

'No. I no longer believe that magic will be bestowed upon me,' he said finally. 'I know it is within me – my birthright – but I need to be certain that I am worthy of it.'

Nat joined us at the edge of the lake. Kneeling, he picked up some loose pebbles. He blew on them and skimmed two across the lake. We watched them fly across the water, skipping two, three and four times. Smiling, he took Pal's hand in his, their fingers interlaced.

Arlene, behind us, began singing. And Nat and Lloyd and Pal all hummed along, deep and low, as she trilled, their notes soaring over the water.

It was as if she were the only person in the world as her rich, steady voice whisked through the trees, arched through the reeds . . . bounded across the lake. Arlene glowed with the beauty of a thousand suns. Once she'd finished, we clapped.

'What magic you weave with your song, young miss!' Pal exclaimed. 'Please!' he implored, stretching his arms out in front of him, sleeves dripping. 'Lady of the Lake, hear our plea! As you gave the sword to Arthur, now assist me and my band of Roamers. The doorway has been breached. I have warriors in training here, but we need weapons, enchanted for their protection. We fight in the name of all that is brave and true.'

The wind skittered through the reeds, causing a stirring and fluttering. The fir trees surrounding the lake rustled and I stared up at them, lifting my chin to the wind, the fresh breeze on my cheeks. The trees moved as one, back and forth, the wind tearing through them, their leaves moving like the waves of the roaring sea. They stood tall and old, ancient and wise, individual, but moving as one; working in harmony, together.

We could do the same.

'Look!' Nat said, pointing.

We stared at the centre of the lake. Ripples quivered outwards, as if from hundreds of skimming stones, and then a column of light beamed up into the sky, as if someone was shining a golden torch from under the water.

The light was white and dazzling, so bright that Lloyd and I squinted, unable to look directly at it.

'Is she there?' I cried out. 'The Lady of the Lake?'

We stood on the shore of the lake and the air warmed around us. The surface of the water eddied, like the beginning of a little whirlpool.

'Do you see that?' I nudged Lloyd.

'Yes. It's like – what *is* that?'

'A sword?' Nat said, jumping up and down. 'Look how shiny it is!'

'Wow,' Arlene breathed, eyes wide.

The tip of a sword, sparkling silver, came out of the column of light. It tipped flat and then floated towards us, bobbing up and down, glinting in the sun's rays.

Glimmers of star fragments, like the sparks of fireworks, rained down around us and danced out from the middle of the lake, skittering across the water like diamonds, sparkling all the way to the shore.

The whirlpool spread out until the whole lake shone with different colours glistening across the water. One by one, items emerged and floated towards us: the sword was followed by an axe with a golden blade, a copper spear and a bow with a quiver of arrows of the deepest turquoise sea-green.

Five butterflies appeared from nowhere and fluttered around each of our heads. Nat laughed and waved at them. They fluttered their colourful wings, shimmering brighter than any I'd seen before – swirly patterns of purples and turquoises, reds, oranges and blues.

'Oh!' Arlene's eyes brimmed with radiance, and she gasped. 'To think they were only caterpillars once!'

We stood there for a while, gazing at the dissolving column of light and the butterflies and dragonflies skittering about. The wind died down as if a mighty voice had called out, *Hush, hush*. The fir trees slowed their swaying and the reeds stilled.

Lloyd leaned over to me and whispered, 'I . . . I don't want to fight, H.'

I swallowed. 'I think we might have to.'

I looked him square in the eye. I wanted to hug him but didn't trust myself not to cry if I did. 'Lloyd. Fighting's not just about wars and guns and bombs, you know. We're not going to hurt anyone on purpose. We can use our brains to outwit them. We can fight by not giving up and sticking together, right?'

He licked his dry lips. 'What if . . .' He cleared his throat and his voice cracked. 'But what if one of us gets hurt?'

'If that happens – we'll all be together, like you said. You're our rock, always steady and sure. Choosing the right path, knowing what's best to do and where to go. Even when we feel lost.'

I made my hope weightier than his doubt.

So many had given up on us – Mum not well enough to stand up against the System, or her own parents, to fight for me; Arlene's mum letting her sadness take over; time stealing Lloyd's grampy's memories ... and Nat, little Nat, with Fablehouse being the only home he'd ever known. No one was taking this from us.

No *one*.

'We can't do it without you.' I grabbed Lloyd's hand and squeezed his fingers. 'We ain't giving up!'

He looked down at my hand, his breath hitched.

'No. We're not.' He squeezed back and smiled, and it was like seeing a rainbow after the rain.

* * *

As the light faded and gave way to a pinky dusk, we gathered up the weapons. On the way back to the moorland, Pal sidled alongside me. The others were far ahead, Lloyd carrying the sword and bow, Arlene the spear and Nat the axe, chattering, full of plans of what we could do and how we were going to rescue everyone, but my heart felt bruised and my feet like lead. Could we do this? I knew we had to try.

Pal put his hand on my shoulder. 'You have great anger inside you, Heather.'

I shook him off, irritated.

'No, I don't.'

He gave me a knowing smile. 'Yes, you do. I know because I recognise it.'

'So what?' I squashed my hands into fists. 'We wouldn't even be in this danger if we lived with our real parents! It's so unfair.'

'You're right.' He nodded. 'Life *is* unfair. Sometimes you can behave correctly and still go unrecognised and unnoticed.' He stopped walking then and wound his hair ropes into a bundle at the back of his head. 'But you do not do the right thing to be thanked, or applauded, you do the right thing because it is *the right thing*.'

I didn't need another lecture on how anger was unbecoming in a young lady. I'd heard that often enough.

'I *feel* your anger and understand it. Do not be ashamed of it or feel you need to hide it. But you must use it as fuel, as passion. As energy and agency for change. Don't let it destroy you, because if you aren't careful—'

'What?' I snapped.

'If you aren't careful ... that anger can fester. I

watched many noble men, knights, give in to their anger and it destroyed them. But anger, rage even, in and of itself, is neither to be feared nor ignored. Respect it, but most importantly – understand where it is coming from. Always speak your rage aloud, direct it outwards, use it. Fire burns bright.'

'You sound so calm! As if it's easy to be noble,' I said, turning my face away, glad that the sky was darkening. 'But what about you? Aren't you angry?'

'I am. Merlin broke his promise. He told me if I was loyal, then my powers, my magic, would be revealed. But I have waited. And I have prayed. I have walked on this earth amongst the trees and spoken to the night. There is nothing. No power has been bestowed upon me; no great gifts are waiting to be collected.'

'Why did you believe him?' I hissed. 'You should know you can only trust yourself.'

He bowed his head, his voice so low I had to strain to hear him.

'Merlin said my true power would be felt across landscapes, across generations. He was the wise one to whom everyone looked up. Of course I believed him.

And I desperately wanted to belong, to feel a part of something. What other choice did I have?'

His eyes clouded over. 'I was used to being jeered at by other knights, told I didn't belong at their table. Told that I wasn't worthy, wasn't really one of them. No matter how many beasts I'd slain or how many maidens I rescued. I had to do twice as much as even the weakest, the most pathetic ... And *still* they viewed me with derision. Somehow, they always found a way to make it sound as if what I'd achieved was only by chance. No one acknowledged the great efforts ...'

He pounded his fist into his other hand. 'When Merlin needed a knight to slumber, to be suspended in time, I thought that would be an opportunity to prove my worth.'

I thought of how I'd tried, over the years, to prove myself. To be good enough. And I never was, so I'd stopped trying.

'Sometimes ...' My voice dipped as I started to speak, my eyes shut tight to block out the world. Could I say this to Pal? *Yes.* I could say these words to a knight.

'Sometimes I'm so frightened, Pal. I don't belong anywhere. I don't fit in. No one will ever want me. I'm just no good – probably rotten inside. Maybe it's my fault that Mum got sick, maybe it was me. I think I'm safer on my own, but that's so . . . lonely.'

Suddenly Pal's arms were wrapped around me. He crushed me to him, my cheek scraping his coarse bristles. I felt his heart thudding in his chest. 'It is true that we enter into this world on our own, little one, and we leave on our own too – but you are *not* alone. To think that you are is the world's cruellest trick. More connects us than divides us. Along life's journey, if we are pure of heart and honest in spirit, we can touch many. You never know whose life you might light up with a gentle smile or a kind word. We can forge paths which run alongside one another's, even if we are not always together.'

I nodded. Pal was telling me that although sometimes I felt weighed down by my loneliness, we weren't alone, even when it seemed as if we were. And I thought of the past few days at Fablehouse, being with the others, just listening to the wireless or laying the table, cleaning out the chickens – even doing these little things in silence, felt less lonely.

Pal smiled. 'I feel a tingle in my stomach, much like that beefy spread upon my lips. I cannot wait to see how you Roamers surprise me! Let us train!'

* * *

We stopped in a clearing, a patch of moorland where we could see the cairn but were a little way away from it.

Pal indicated we should all set down the weapons we'd been carrying. Lloyd put down the sword, somewhat reluctantly.

'Beware of the Champion, Mark. He can demand that the earth itself twists and spins. He will use rotten tricks and does not care who he hurts. He will not play fair. But you have been gifted enchanted weapons; they will protect you. They will not cause mortal wounds. We do not have the right to take any lives, human or otherwise.'

Lloyd exhaled loudly in relief.

'Now, these weapons will see whether you are worthy of them. Breathe deeply. Listen to your heartbeat. Feel the earth under your feet. Then choose the weapon which most draws you. If you are quiet and give yourselves time, your weapon will call to you.'

Lloyd, Arlene, Nat and I stood in front of the weapons which Pal had laid on the ground. We looked at each other a little shyly, none of us keen to take the first step, trying to feel our way into the music that the weapons silently played for us.

I felt something shift inside me, like waves rolling. A clang of steel. A flash of iron over a searing charcoal fire.

Humming, Arlene moved forward, and her hand hovered over the axe. Her fingers caressed the splintered wooden handle. 'This has my name on it.' She grinned.

Lloyd stepped forward and picked up the sword. I felt a stab of injustice before he turned to me, brandishing it.

'This whispered your name to me, H,' he said, handing the sword over. I took it, nodding – it was weighty, but it still felt good and solid in my hands. As if I could slice through anything. As I turned it over, the light caught its tip and dazzled silver.

Pal undid his leather harness and handed it to me. 'Wear this well,' he said. 'Your sword can go into this scabbard when you do not need to use it.'

Lloyd picked up the spear, striking it down into the ground at his feet. The copper gleamed.

Pal looked upon us all. 'That leaves the bow for you, young Nat,' he said.

Nat's eyes twinkled as if he had just been given a Christmas present.

'And there we have my band of Roamers. My wandering warriors.'

A big smile crossed Pal's face as he spread out his arms. 'Now, to practise!'

* * *

We spent hours listening and learning from Pal. The weapons became natural extensions of us, almost responding to our thoughts, as well as our touch. I knew they were enchanted, but they seemed to work with us too. It was as if I'd always known how to carry and brandish a sword. I couldn't imagine the others without their weapons either.

Whenever I wielded the sword, it suddenly became light and at times the blade appeared to be almost liquid, the way it would bend and extend much further from where I thought I'd aimed.

We dodged and weaved until we could barely see any longer. Pal taught us how to duck and parry. Arlene threw her axe, spinning it through the air before always landing only inches away from someone's ear, whistling as it went.

I balanced an apple on top of Pal's head. 'Don't move!'

He sat cross-legged with a solemn expression as Nat took aim with his bow. He drew an arrow back, released, and we gasped as it zipped through the air, swerving to puncture the apple right through.

'Whoo-hoo!' Nat hollered, dropping the bow, and jumping up and down. 'See that? See what I did?'

'Indeed!' Pal laughed. 'A true aim!'

His laugh was rich and thundered up through the soles of my feet until it echoed deep in my own chest, and then the chests of everyone else. Here we all were – right here, right now; the warrior Roamers, about to go on our quest!

Lloyd launched fallen twigs and branches into the air and every time I swiped, I'd catch a branch right in the middle and two halves fell perfectly either side of me.

'You're lucky!' cried Nat, clapping.

But luck had nothing to do with it. I wasn't making any decisions on when to swipe, or which direction to lean into. Something else guided me, a deep-seated, long-buried instinct.

'Well.' Pal stretched his neck, and shook his hair ropes loose. They whipped back and forth. 'We will rest a while. Your training is as complete as it can be.'

'We're ready?' Nat asked, looking at us with his eyebrows raised.

Arlene gulped. 'Really?'

'Your weapons are strong, and you are keen. There is nothing more I can teach you. You may need to use your wits with the Champion. Don't only rely on your weapons. He is big but slow. You are nimble and fast-thinking, which may work to your advantage. Remember what makes you Roamers.'

We stared at each other, our smiles and good mood suddenly replaced by nerves and the under-standing of what we were about to do.

Lloyd said, 'Let's go.'

Taking a big, brave breath, I smiled at Nat and Arlene, who both looked wide-eyed.

'I'm frightened,' Arlene blurted out. The hand holding her axe shook and she dropped it.

'That's all right,' I said, giving her my best smile. 'I am a bit too.'

'An' me!' Nat squeaked. 'I don't feel very brave.'

'Being brave doesn't mean you're not afraid,' Lloyd said softly, his eyes shining. 'I think being brave is going ahead and doing it anyway, even with the fear there, like when Grampy had to move into the home.'

'It is time,' Pal said, clapping his hand on Lloyd's shoulder. 'Battle is never easy, but I have never seen braver knights than you! Trust your hearts and each other.'

Chapter Fourteen

Fae Feld

'It's up to us now,' I said, picking up Arlene's axe and handing it to her. 'No one else is coming.' I put my hand on her shoulder and patted it. 'We can do this.'

'But we aren't the Chosen!' she whimpered, shaking me off. 'We'll end up trapped down there forever!' She dashed away the tears brimming in her eyes. 'Why don't you all go, and I'll wait here with Pal.'

Nat shook his head, biting his lip. 'I know it's scary . . . but I think Heather's right. We have to . . . *try*. And it's got to be the four of us – right, Lloyd? Pal?'

Pal and Lloyd looked at each other. Pal raised his eyebrows and nodded at the same time as Lloyd raised his spear, pressed his lips together and said, 'We do have to try.'

Ahead of us, the sky was gloomy and brooding. It felt like it was going to rain, the clouds low and heavy. The cairn stones, once piled so high in a magnificent tower, now lay broken and scattered in a huge pile, like a giant had just kicked his way through them. A hazy heat flicker wavered across the top of the stones, casting mysterious shadows over them.

As we walked forward, stepping closer to the centre where the stones had been, it was as if something, or someone, held us back, a swell of unyielding pressure at our waists.

'What's the matter?' Nat asked, frowning. 'Why can't we get any closer?' He leaned forward, shoulders squared, but still couldn't move.

Pal crouched, tilted his head, and peered along the ground. The hazy flicker shifted and wavered and lowered itself to his eyeline.

''Tis enchanted,' Pal said simply. 'Look.' He gestured around the haze, and we squatted low. Peering upwards, I could see a faint purple line shimmering all around.

'A Fae force field.' Pal sat on the heathland, pushing aside a pile of stones. He sighed. 'We won't be able to pass through – they have protected their realm well. I am at a loss as to how we can proceed.' He rubbed a hand across his face.

Was this it then? The end even before we'd begun? *No way.* Not on my watch. I gritted my teeth, nearly growling. 'Come on, we must be able to do something!'

Lloyd shrugged. 'Like what, H?'

'I don't know!'

We glanced around at the bigger rocks at our feet. Nat pointed to a loose slab, and with both hands picked it up. 'See this one? It's got a pattern on it.'

I sheathed my sword and took the slab off him, peering at it. Nat was right. Spirals were etched into both sides. Examining them, I turned over the stone in my hands. 'Reminds me of a snail shell.'

Arlene came over to look. 'So pretty!'

'Isn't it?' As I tilted the slab, the deep grooves caught the light and glinted a greeny shine. The slab was smooth and flat, covered in overlapping circles – a design too neat to be an accident.

'It probably means something?' Lloyd said.

Now all of us stared at the stone I held.

'Yeah, but what?' I traced my fingers in the deep furrows. The hollows were grainy under my fingertips, and when I looked at my fingers, they were stained green, the whorls of my fingerprints standing out.

'What do you think?' I held it out to Pal. 'Looks like the symbols in the grimoire.'

Pal jumped up. I handed him the stone and he wrapped his fist around it. We watched him take a few deep breaths before closing his eyes. The air around us grew very still and peaceful.

'I believe this is an ancient sign, connected to Fae magic. I have seen something similar before, on coats of arms, but –' he cast his eyes around at our feet – 'this is only part of something bigger. There may be other stones like this. We should try to find them; they are talismans.'

We laid our weapons down and bent over, raking through the piles of different-sized stones gathered around our feet. I sorted through a small pile in front of me. Most stones we upturned were plain, but Nat quickly found another, and after a while both Arlene and Lloyd yelled, 'Here!'

'Mine has the same design as yours, H, like a mirror image,' Lloyd said, showing me his stone, triangular but with edges worn smooth; it had similar swirls and spirals.

'Wait!' said Pal, reaching down and handing me back my stone. 'Roamers, have you all found marked stones?'

We looked at each other, held up our stones and nodded. Pal closed his fist and put his hand across his chest, as if taking a vow.

'Close your fists around the stones. Now, remember that the four of you – together – are stronger than each of you alone. This is sacred land. The land of a thousand knights, the scenes of many hard-won battles. Focus on gaining entry. You deserve to find your friends. Be warriors of spirit.'

Stood almost in a circle, we held the stones and concentrated. I didn't know what this would do, but as Nat said, we had to try.

The words of the grimoire rattled through my mind. *Your friends are at the mercy of the Fae leader. There is only one way to get them back. Fae Feld awaits the brave and true.*

'My stone's getting warm!' Nat exclaimed suddenly.

'Mine too!' said Arlene.

'Keep hold of them!' Pal shouted. 'Even if they get hot, try to keep hold.'

I cracked one eye open and saw a glow pulsing around the stones in our hands. It was almost like chalk dust. The grooves glowed and tiny cracks appeared, feathering outwards, like cracks in glass.

'Pal!' Lloyd called, a sudden wild wind almost drowning out his words. His short hair whipped back and forth. 'What's happening?'

Arlene and I struggled to keep our balance.

'Something's pulling me!' Nat swayed.

The wind swallowed Pal's words. 'The land, I think... it recognises you as knights... Now, go forth to the centre of the cairn!'

With Lloyd in front, we followed – whatever force field was present before now letting us through – stumbling over loose stones, still clutching ours, along with our weapons.

The stones, where the middle of the cairn had been, spread outwards, crawling over one another and forming a circle around a moss-covered empty space. As we got closer, the previous feeling of pressure fell further away, and there was now a circular scorch mark burned into the ground. Stood close together, we just about fitted inside the circle.

'Well, I guess X marks the—'

Lloyd didn't finish his sentence as the earth under our feet shifted and fell away. 'Whoa!' he cried, steadying himself as we sank a foot into the ground. We huddled closer, frantically glancing around to see Pal.

'What's happening?' I shouted, trying to keep my balance, but the ground lurched again, and I slammed into Nat. 'Sorry!'

The earth swelled and then crumpled under our feet, like a tablecloth being yanked away.

'Pal!' Nat yelled.

Pal's hair ropes whipped in the wind. 'I cannot approach!' he shouted.

We watched him try to step forward, head bent, shoulders braced, but it was as if invisible hands held him back. Grimacing, he strained against something none of us could see.

'Ahh!' We dropped down another foot.

'We're sinking!' cried Arlene, her knuckles turning white as she gripped her axe.

All around where the centre of the cairn had been, the ground sank, as a sinkhole suddenly appeared. We craned our necks to peer upwards.

Pal stared down at us. 'I cannot cross this threshold, my Roamers.'

We were descending deep into the ground.

Arlene moaned. 'Any last-minute advice?'

'Don't trust all you see,' he replied. 'Rescue requires resistance!'

The ground groaned under us. Clods of earth from above tumbled into the hole, and we ducked and covered our heads.

'We should wait till Pal figures out how to come too,' Nat said, his voice trembling.

'We don't have a choice – we're moving!' I said firmly.

Lloyd nodded. 'H is right. We need to find Miss Isolde and the others!'

'Pal – will you still be here?' Nat cried out, as the ground kept crumbling around us. We kept descending and Pal became smaller and smaller.

'I shall protect the grimoire!' Pal shouted down into the abyss. 'I shall not move.'

He leaned over the hole, his hair ropes swinging back and forth. Part of me wanted to catch hold of one and haul myself out of this hole. *What were we heading towards?*

'It is clear that I am allowed no further! This quest is for you now.' He nodded gravely. 'Go wise and go well, warriors.'

Chapter Fifteen

A New World

No going back now.

Clustered together, gripping each other, the section of earth we stood on groaned, as if we were too heavy for it, and, juddering, sank further and further down. As we sank deeper, clods of mud crumbled and fell on to us. Arlene squealed, shaking off a shiny beetle that had landed on her shoulder. Falling at her feet, its body flashed with a spark of blue light before, wriggling, it disappeared back into the earth.

Tree roots at the sides arched and snapped off, leaving frayed twigs which scraped our cheeks, like sharp spindly fingers reaching for us.

We're stronger together, we're stronger together, I kept thinking over and over.

We eyed each other silently, lips pressed tightly together to keep out the dirt. Arlene clamped her eyes shut and I watched, transfixed, as her lips moved rapidly. I knew she was silently praying. Nat's fingers closed around my hand, and even though he was crushing it, I didn't say anything. His eyes flickered around, wide and scared.

From beneath us came a rhythmic, steady rumbling, like a drum repeatedly being struck. The hairs on my arms shivered to attention, the beating making my insides vibrate. The sound called to me somehow, gave me images of campfires and flames. Of warmth and light.

Lloyd's jaw was set firm, and I knew by how his muscles flexed that he was grinding his teeth.

The temperature dropped, and the opening above us became no bigger than a pinprick, and shadows rolled in from all around. I stared at our chance to escape, our chance to recognise anything normal ever again, vanishing before me.

Where were we and what were we doing?

Pal wasn't with us! We were on our own.

My eyes gradually adjusted to the dimness. Dank earth pressed against our backs, giving way to high walls of slick, packed mud. A scuttling, like hundreds of insects running up the columns of mud, grew louder, though I couldn't see anything.

'I'm scared!' Nat said, shivering along with the quiver of arrows on his back.

Lloyd and I glanced at Nat and Arlene. 'Stick together and we'll be OK,' I said, not knowing if I believed the words coming out of my own mouth; I just knew Arlene and Nat were both frightened. Even if we didn't feel brave, we had to act it – I knew that much.

'I wonder how far we're going down,' Lloyd murmured, his eyes not quite meeting mine, mud and twigs in his hair.

'Feels like we're travelling to the bottom of the world.' Nat gulped. He turned to Arlene, and she put her arm around him and hummed comfortingly in his ear.

But then the ground under our feet shuddered and we suddenly jerked to a stop. There was almost a growl as the ground squelched.

The packed sides of mud smashed apart and returned to the earth. Fae Feld opened out. In front of us was a long narrow pathway, lined either side with overhanging bare tree branches. I listened. None of us moved. The air buzzed with whispers announcing our arrival, and everything seemed alive in this realm ... the ground itself breathing, sucking and heaving. I felt sharper somehow, my senses tingling. Everything seemed ... *more*, down here.

I shuffled over and muttered to Lloyd, 'Do you feel all right?'

'Think so, why?' Lloyd stared at me for a while. He raised his eyebrows. 'You OK?'

I gripped the handle of my sword. The cool metal hilt reassured me. 'I think so. I'm not sure.' Apart from my quickening heartbeat and flutters in my stomach, I wasn't sure how else to explain what I was feeling. It was as if my head had been plunged into freezing water; my scalp tingled.

I cricked my neck. 'I feel really ... *awake*.'

The atmosphere was strange. The air felt thick and not clean enough to breathe. Like if you took a deep breath, something might sneak its way into your mouth. The place felt charged with life; you could almost hear heartbeats and squeaking and snuffling, and yet there was no sign of life anywhere. I'd never seen such a variety of plants and flowers and leaves, but didn't recognise any. They weren't like the wild-flowers in Fablehouse's garden, where brightness lifted everyone. There was no joy here, only a heavy, over-perfumed misery; cloying, as if someone were trying to cover up a bad smell with an even worse one.

This place seemed to be half-swamp and half-jungle. An eerie green glow came from underneath giant leaves which sprouted up from the ground. Their roots were fat tubes, and their leaves half an inch thick and wider than my outstretched arms. They looked big enough to hold Nat, should he choose to sit in the middle of them.

We all looked at each other. None of us stepped forward.

Nat wrinkled his nose. 'What's that smell?'

I breathed in deeply: smouldering bonfires and rotting leaves, pine cones and the sickly sweetness of dying roses. The smell of wet earth was intense. Like when the soil has been overturned – dense and dark.

'Lloyd?' Nat whimpered, his voice small. 'Are they – are those ... *bones*?' His fingers trembled as he pointed to a pile off to one side.

'Just white birch twigs, Nat,' Lloyd replied softly.

Nat's breath was sharp. 'But they're *moving...*'

'It's the wind,' Lloyd said.

I glanced at the hedges and rustling leaves, maybe once green, but now scorched yellow and brown. 'There is no wind ... because there's no sky, no sun. Look up.'

Instead of sky, the air was filled with a green-tinged mist. It reminded me of eating Quality Street at Christmas time and staring through the brightly coloured clear wrappers, changing the colours of the world.

'And I think ... I think *everything is m-moving*,' I stuttered, 'because it's all – it's all *alive*.'

Thick vegetation surrounded us; more huge leaves, some with bleached-out spirals on them, others with spiky, jagged edges. They fanned out in every direction, bending and waving, all tinged various shades of green, yellow and brown.

'It's magic then,' Nat whispered. 'Real magic.'

'It's life,' I said simply, gazing open-mouthed at a line of enormous snails, each as big as dinner plates, trudging into the undergrowth, their shells lined with scratches and scars, the trails they left glittering silver and green.

Arlene shuddered. 'They're awful!' She coughed. 'I wish I'd brought something to – ooh, apples!' She reached over to a tree, but I batted her arm down.

'Careful! Haven't you read enough fairy tales?' I said sharply, before she could pluck an apple off a branch.

'I wasn't going to eat one,' she griped. 'I just wanted a look. Anyway, there are maggots coming out of them – look!'

Fat maggots curled up and out of the misshapen apples, white, like wriggling lines of chalk, against the mossy green.

'What should we do?' Lloyd glanced around.

I put my hand on the top of my sword in its sheath. 'Find our friends and avoid this Champion.'

Arlene sighed. 'Any idea how we do that?'

I couldn't answer, but sensed the others behind me. Something was off down here. I could smell it – fear and misery. *Which way?* I needed to see what Fae Feld held, what we might have to face.

As we moved forward, gnarled, ancient tree stumps clung to the uneven ground, blackened and writhing slowly. Furry moss and stringy vines swung from branches, dangling to strangle tree trunks. Mounds of termite nests clung to branches and lichen crackled, covering every surface. Steam, or smoke, sprang from clumps of earth, which belched out more sickly-sweet smells.

Every step we took, vines threaded their way into our hair, but it didn't feel like they were trying to stop us, just that this world was curious about who we were and why we were there. Almost as if they were reaching out somehow ...

'Wh-what's that noise?' Arlene gulped, and grabbed my elbow.

There were snuffles and grunts and snorts, a scampering of feet, but nothing crossed our path. I kicked a rotten apple core crawling with blood-red ants. Arlene stepped into a pile of mulchy leaves which squelched underfoot.

Now the air appeared even dimmer. I strained to

see clearly in front of me, stooping under branches. I didn't like this. It felt like everything was crowding in on us. Watching us. We were too exposed here. Would the Champion know we were coming? Had someone told him? We needed to get moving. We needed to hurry.

'Lloyd, which way do you ...' but his expression made me stop still.

He'd stuck his spear into the ground and was now staring at that spot, transfixed.

'Nat, Arlene, H – can you see this?' Lloyd beckoned us towards him.

He crouched and pushed his fingers through the earth. As the dirt collected underneath his fingernails, his eyes widened.

'Have you dropped something?' Nat asked, getting on his hands and knees to help.

'No, no,' Lloyd said, standing up straight. 'Nothing like that.' He pointed at the ground, his hand shaking. 'I don't know what's happening, but can you see a sort of ... trail?'

'A what?' Arlene stared at his trembling fingers.

I stepped up to where he was. 'A trail?'

'I see footprints.' Lloyd cleared his throat and looked at me. 'An outline of Miss Isolde's boot. It's shimmering and glowing. It's like I'm being shown – I don't know – a trace.' He gestured towards the ground, but all I saw were puddles full of algae.

Nat frowned at Arlene's confused expression. 'What do you mean?'

Lloyd wrinkled his nose, trying to find the right words. 'When we cleared the stables for Pal, and shook out those old sacks, little bits flew up into the air, didn't they? Or, you know when it's sunny and specks of dust catch the sunlight? It looks a bit like that.'

I said, 'You think it's showing you where people went?'

'I think so. I can't quite explain. It's like the foot-prints someone *would* leave behind, but now they're sort of dimples in the air. But I don't understand why you lot can't see anything!'

But I'd seen the changelings first when no one else had been able to. Maybe Lloyd could see things that the rest of us couldn't too?

'We are in another realm here,' I said quietly.

'Another world. Things are bound to be different, aren't they? Let's say you *can* see something – go ahead – just lead the way. We'll follow.'

Lloyd offered me a grateful smile. 'Yes. Maybe I'm seeing it for a reason, especially if none of you can. Something about here feels really ... familiar. What did Pal say? As *above, so below*? Well, it's like I've been here before. Maybe I can work out the best way for us to go. Like I do above?'

That sounded possible.

We all fell silent again, listening to our own heart-beats, our own thoughts. Lloyd led the way, with me behind, and we walked quietly, warily, weapons in hand. My fingers kept straying to the tip of my sword, resting lightly on the cold metal, checking it was still there.

Even though up above it was summer, down here it felt more like autumn; muggy, but with a winter crispness hovering close by. Twigs cracked; mounds of earth slunk along the ground. I glimpsed flashes of glowing eyes, peeking out from the undergrowth. But nothing made any move towards us.

Were these the Fae? Creatures that clearly

blended in with the earth? Every time I noticed a leaf or flower I'd never seen before, it scuttled away, bristling.

'I can't work them out,' I whispered, nudging Lloyd. 'I feel as if I'm being watched, don't you?'

Lloyd raised his eyebrows. 'Definitely. But they seem . . . cautious. It's not what I was expecting.'

'This place gives me the creeps!' hissed Arlene, behind me. 'Glassy eyes everywhere, it's spooky!'

Nat squeaked, 'We're in another land! What did you expect?'

I tramped down hard on the narrow loose dirt path in front of us. 'I don't know, but I wish we could *see* who we're facing . . .' I sighed. Where was everyone from Fablehouse? How were we ever going to find them!

'Those eyes glare like something unholy,' muttered Arlene. 'Look at them shine!' She stared at the eyes lighting up the dense bushes and hedgerows lining our path.

She was right. All around was like when you see cats or foxes at night and their eyes catch the light strangely and look just like mirrors.

'Is it a trick?' she asked. 'Think they're waiting to attack?'

'Maybe not,' I said suddenly. 'What if they're scared of us?'

They watched me with questioning expressions on their faces.

'In our world, people aren't just one thing or the other, are they? You're not all good or all bad, are you? Well, maybe the Fae are like that too? The grimoire said the Fae were under the Champion's control ... that he'd made them promises. Maybe it's hard to resist, if someone offers you everything you ever wanted.'

'H is right,' Lloyd said. 'We can't judge a whole tree just because of one or two rotten apples. Maybe there are some Fae who might help us.'

'Pfft.' Arlene crinkled her nose. 'If they want to help, then why won't they show themselves? Seems to me like these lot are hiding something, or else why not come out? Why would they blindly follow this Champion?'

'Maybe they don't have a choice,' muttered Nat.

'Well, I don't trust them!' Arlene pushed past me to be behind Lloyd. 'Can you still see this trail?'

'Yes.' Lloyd slammed his spear into the ground. 'Here reminds me of the way to the cairn. I think everywhere down here is exactly like our land, laid out like Fablehouse . . .'

'Let's keep moving then,' Arlene said as she swung her axe through the branches hanging in our way.

We followed behind her as she cleared a path, still looking all around us. Branches splintered and the air tensed as if someone were pinching it. We each caught our breath sharply as spores flared up, like when you've blown a dandelion and made a wish. As I watched them float above us, they sizzled, and green and blue flames sparkled before fizzling out. They were oddly, mesmerisingly beautiful.

'See those? Now, *that's* magic.' Smiling, I turned to Nat, but he wasn't anywhere to be seen.

Chapter Sixteen

The Temptations

'Nat!' I called, spinning round and scanning the path behind us. Was it my imagination, or had the leaves and bushes grown and moved, blocking our view? Blooming fatter somehow? Had the Fae made that happen? Maybe Arlene was right, and they didn't deserve to be trusted. What if they were biding their time, planning to attack?

Whatever hold the Champion had over them, the Fae had taken our friends and now one of the Roamers too!

'Lloyd!' I cried out. 'Wait – Nat's disappeared!'

'That way!' Lloyd pointed off to the right, but all

I could see was a tangle of low bushes. I winced; they looked thorny.

'How do you know?' Arlene asked.

'The trace! I can see a different one for Nat somehow. The earth is showing me where he's been.'

A low mist swirled up from the ground, whirling around our heads. I swiped at it with my arms. It felt deliberate now, like something or someone was trying to stop us seeing what was up ahead.

'Nat!' Arlene shouted. 'Where are you?'

'Can you hear that?' I held up my hand and we stopped moving. 'Nat?'

Faint laughter came from a distance away. I ran forward, ahead of Lloyd, splashing through deeper puddles, duckweed and fronds clinging to my boots, and saw Nat in a small clearing, kneeling on the ground with his back to me.

'Nat!' I yelled. My racing heartbeat slowed down; I was so relieved to see him!

But he didn't turn around, just sat there in the mulch and mud, chattering away to what looked like a rotten tree stump.

'Quick!' I beckoned to the others.

'Eww! What *is* that?' Arlene recoiled and wrinkled her nose as she ducked behind me.

As we got closer, it was obvious that Nat wasn't looking at a tree stump at all. Something, about the size of a big dog, stood on its hind legs; something that perhaps might have been a hare once, but was now more like several animals stitched together. Whatever it was had the thick whip-like tail of a rat, long pointed ears which were torn and matted, caked with blood or mud, and thorns poking out of its brown, patchy-furred stomach. Was this what the Questing Beast had looked like?

'*Oh,*' Nat exhaled dreamily, gesturing in front of him. 'Look! Isn't that the fluffiest bunny you've ever seen?' His face was full of light, his big brown eyes shining unnaturally bright, like they'd been polished. 'Its fur is like snow!'

He smiled and nodded at it, as if listening. 'It wants to take us to a feast being held especially in our honour! There will be cakes and meat pies and sweets and—'

'Heather!' cried Arlene, alongside me, tugging on my arm. 'That's no bunny! What's *wrong* with him? Why is he saying all that?'

I glanced around; emerald eyes shimmered from bushes in the distance. Wisps of green smoke and dark fronds, like slimy tendrils, slithered out of the creature's stomach, reaching towards Nat, who gazed up at it like it was the cutest animal he'd ever seen.

'Not sure.' Lloyd shook his head. 'I think he's seeing something different to what we are.'

Fae can make us see whatever they want us to see ...

We stared at Nat trying to pet this horrible creature, smiling and chattering serenely to himself, all the while smoke snaking its way around him, funnelling its way into his ears and up his nose. We had to get him away from it.

'Heather – shock him out of it!' Arlene begged.

I remembered how my anger had burst open the lock on the grimoire. I tried to get angry; there was enough to be angry about – the Fae taking away everything we cared for, the Champion who had set this whole plan in motion for his own gain, us Roamers facing this all alone – but before I could reach Nat, Lloyd stepped firmly in between us.

'I don't think we should touch him – who knows what that might do,' he said, his voice sure and comforting. 'But let me try something, H.' He went and put his face close to the back of Nat's head, his lips almost touching his ear.

I stepped back, my anger only faintly stirring anyway because I was scared and sad, not cross.

'Nat? This isn't real,' Lloyd whispered in his ear. 'There isn't a friendly, fluffy white rabbit in front of you. The Fae are trying to trick and distract you. You're seeing something that isn't there. And you can't stay. There isn't any feast. We need to get back to Fablehouse, our home. Fablehouse is real. *Remember*.'

Nat's eyes were blank. 'You don't need me. I can stay here. They want me to play.' His voice chilled me; there was no life in it, no joy, no ... *Nat*. Was this how the changelings had taken our friends? By taking the essence of them first? The very thing that made them *them*? I couldn't watch. I clenched my fists and searched the ground for a stone or branch to throw at the repulsive creature.

'We do need you. We love you,' Lloyd urged. 'If you're not with us, who will make us laugh? Who will shine the light when darkness comes? Nat, *you* are our magic.'

Nat tore his eyes away from the shiny smoke and stared at Lloyd. He reached both arms forward, trying to pet the creature, but it wavered and wobbled and collapsed into greeny-grey smoke.

'Can you hear me?' Lloyd put his hand on Nat's shoulder and rubbed it gently.

Nat blinked slowly. The shifting smoke hissed and, snapping, spun up and away from Nat, writhing under bushes.

'Are you listening?' Lloyd asked softly.

Arlene and I reached for one another's hands. Feeling her hand shaking, I squeezed it gently.

Nat looked up at us all suspiciously. 'What ... ?' He began coughing and his face crumpled into tears; the spell had been broken!

'I think you were ... hypnotised,' I said, offering my hand to help pull him up. I turned to Lloyd, to see what he thought, how he might explain it, but he'd stopped short and was staring off into the distance as Arlene and I hugged and comforted a dazed-looking Nat.

'*Grampy?*' Lloyd gasped, delighted.

Nat, still coughing, spluttered, 'Don't breathe in! Hold your breath. There's something in the air, it's what made my mind all dizzy!'

But it was too late for Lloyd. The moment that hope-filled wonder surged into his voice, I knew that the Fae had sunk their claws deep into him. My Lloyd, the person we needed to show us the way; the person I needed to keep me on the straight and true; my compass.

I steeled myself, led Nat over to Arlene and said firmly, 'Right. You both sit together on that log. Cover your mouth and nose. Only look at each other, and just wait for me, OK?'

Arlene trembled, afraid. She clutched her axe in one hand, and with the other grabbed Nat's hand.

'Lloyd?' I said.

He gazed straight through me.

'Yes, these are my new cards. Look!' He spread his hands as if showing someone something. His fingers quivered, dancing to a rhythm of their own.

I went to stand in front of Lloyd and watched his lips moving softly, his voice tender.

What was he seeing? What were the Fae offering?

'Oh yes please, I'd love to play cricket with you. Here, shall I bowl?'

He *was seeing his beloved grampy*. Every word he uttered splintered my heart.

Lloyd's smile was as wide as I'd ever seen it, as he polished an imaginary cricket ball against his trouser leg. As I watched him run up and down, it was as if hands were around my throat, choking the life out of me; long, looming shadows crowded in around me. How could I reach him? I didn't want to shock Lloyd – it seemed wrong somehow, too violent – but I needed him to know that I was here for him, just like he'd been for Nat.

'Lloyd?' I put my hand on his arm.

He glanced at it vaguely, but he wasn't seeing me, and he twitched, shaking me off.

'Grampy!'

The triumph in his voice trembled through the trees and he said it again, loud, and proud, and I hated the Fae with every ounce of my being for the lies they were offering my friend. Lies held up as the truths we all longed for the most.

'Grampy recognises me – he knows my name!' Lloyd said, elated. 'He knows who I am!'

I stifled my sobs because who wouldn't want that?

Suddenly the trees began rustling ... I strained to hear clackety voices overlapping.

You are in our realm now. This is Fae Feld. Our magic is like no other. Ever wish you could undo something you once said, see your loved ones again, start over? Restore what was lost? We can give you all that and more - so much more! What would you like to see?

Tell usssss!

Lloyd sank to his knees, staring up rapturously, as if listening to an almighty choir. I couldn't bear seeing him like this, believing that his precious grampy was well and waiting for him.

I didn't feel myself without Lloyd by my side. But what was the best way to break the spell over him? I didn't have his quiet, soft way of speaking which had worked on Nat. I wasn't gentle and calm; I was the impatient one who rushed, said things without thinking first, and that might be a disaster here.

I saw, by how Lloyd's face shone, by the happy tears in his eyes, how much this meant to him. How much he longed for this vision to be real. I knew he'd lived this dream over and over – being the perfect little English boy, head to toe in cricket whites, fitting in, not looking out of place. He wanted his grampy, but he wanted – like all of us, even if we didn't know it – to belong even more. To be included; wanted for who we were; accepted just as we are.

It was like I could see into him, into the Fae too, suddenly – see how they truly felt and why they felt that way. It was as if everyone's hearts and hurts and hopes were being paraded in front of me.

The quiet sadness that usually shrouded Lloyd like a cloak had vanished, and he looked lighter and brighter, carefree. Who was I to take that away from him?

A lump in my throat swelled and I swallowed.

What would I want Lloyd to do for me, if I was the one trapped like he was? What did he need?

'Lloyd!' I yelled so loud the effort scraped my throat. 'You can't stay here. It's not safe!'

My breath hitched.

Echoes whisked through the trees, shook bare branches. I gazed upwards at glistening, dark green leaves churning around Lloyd's head, almost tickling him.

'None of this is real!'

Tall trees shuddered. The ground under my feet groaned. I stepped backwards and, hearing crunching, I looked down – broken, cracked and split snail shells. Their homes ruined: *just like ours.*

I gasped. *What if* . . . the Fae were the same as us? What if Arlene was wrong and *they* just needed to be understood and appreciated and wanted? What if they'd been treated unfairly and wrongly judged too? No wonder then that they'd be tempted by promises of riches. By promises of a better life, a home which came with freedom. We knew the Champion was behind this, but maybe it went back to Merlin banishing the Fae down here. Who wouldn't feel betrayed by that?

Maybe it wasn't Lloyd I needed to speak to – maybe I needed to appeal to the Fae, get them to understand. I couldn't see any of them, but their presence filled the air.

'Fae, listen to me!' I demanded. 'I know your life is hard, being hidden, staying back . . . I know you've been cheated and lied to. I know you feel abandoned. But whatever you have been told by your master, whatever promises he has made, taking over the human realm is not the way. You cannot take what doesn't belong to you.'

The air whistled and the lights from eyes in the undergrowth winked in and out.

'You don't need whatever the Champion has promised. Riches won't change anything; you don't need jewels and gold. It's *you* who have the real power; there are hundreds of you and only one of him. Don't you know that? Whatever you do for him, he'll always demand more of you! You'll never be able to please him. Living in fear is no way to live. I understand how scared you must be. I lash out sometimes too – when I'm scared or worried. But ask yourselves, deep down, what you *really* want. What's important to you? Listen to your own hearts and each other. You deserve to be free again. But there's no way you're taking Lloyd. He's our friend and I won't let you have him! He's needed here, with us.'

As the words flew from my mouth, they seemed to take on a solid form, smoke buzzing around my lips, bursting into wisps of flame which glided over to Lloyd. They surrounded him in a warm glow.

'Lloyd, come back to me. Please! You always know

what to say and do. You show us all the right way. If you don't come back to us – we'll be lost.' My voice cracked. 'I'll be lost without you!'

My chest heaved. It felt like everything I'd kept locked away, tight and safe inside, had broken free. My feelings of protection and love for Lloyd and the Roamers grew so big they crowded out everything else. Four luminous sparks, shimmering with amber and copper and gold, fanned out on the ground next to me. As my boots touched them, they began to spin, like Catherine wheels of light. Small fireballs took shape and soared into the air. The sparks settled around my head, lighting us all up. Lighting up everything.

Lloyd stared ahead into the darkness but the glow was radiant and threw everything into focus, revealing the truth behind the illusion. His fingers twitched as he dropped his imaginary cricket ball.

'Grampy ... one day, I'll see you again, but not today.'

Even though Lloyd's hands shook, he reached out to my frothing fireballs, the beads of orange light surrounding him. As his fingers made contact, they burst into flame-coloured dust, cobalt flaring, and fizzled through the air.

Then he cried out, a cry full of grief and disappointment and longing – full of everything that meant so much and hurt so deeply. I knew that he'd never be able to express those feelings, because I often felt the same. Those words didn't exist yet. You could only share those feelings by a look or a nod, by a smile or a hug.

'Fae!' His voice came, deadly calm and formidable. 'Your magic comes at a cost, and us Roamers will have no part in it. Your trickery and lies make you no better than the Champion. Know this: you cannot break our bond of friendship apart! Together we are as strong as any army. Whatever Grampy's future may be – the Fae have no say in it.'

Although he sounded determined, his eyes had clouded over even before he'd finished speaking.

'Oh, Lloyd,' I said, barely able to see through my brimming tears. I went to him and picked up his spear, which had fallen on the ground. 'That must have been tough.' I pushed the curls back off his forehead.

He stumbled into a tree stump and gripped the bark for support. Breathing hard, he leaned against the tree and hung his head – hands over his face. I stood next to him, watching and waiting.

What had it taken for him to come out of that Fae trance?

When he looked up at me, I handed him his spear. He clung to it, his eyes clear now and full of purpose.

'We need to find Arlene and Nat. Us Roamers need to stick together and keep on moving before they trick us again. The sooner we can return to Fablehouse the better.'

Chapter Seventeen

The Illusion of the Imaginary

I was glad to have Lloyd back with us. The Fae's tricks had stopped us from focusing. We needed to use Lloyd's tracking powers to get back to following Miss Isolde's tracks in the . . .

'Heffver?'

Who was that?

'Heffver, *help!*'

My ears tingled, prickled. I spun around, trying to get my bearings. Where had that voice come from?

Davey?

Davey needed me! A clump of tall fir trees parted as I turned to dash through the middle of them. They closed behind me with barely a whisper. I looked around. I didn't recognise anything. I twirled in a circle, surrounded by trees packed together, a wall of moving green, with small gaps between them that led off in different directions.

'Davey!' I shouted, cupping my hands round my mouth. I strained, listening for a response.

'Heffver ... !' There it was again, faint but there. I rushed forward through another group of trees which led out on to a wider path, before swishing closed behind me.

'Where are you?' Panicking, I spun around, trees towering around me, swaying. I couldn't see past or through them. They quivered together, flowing as one, like a living, breathing wave.

Sea trees, I thought, staring up at them. Just like at the lake, they waved their branches, creating a rhythm I couldn't take my eyes off, all fluttering together. The sound was so peaceful that I found myself swaying along with it until I felt as if I were floating. I wanted to sit down for a moment to listen ... to let the soothing sounds wash over me.

The smell of warm spices drifted in the air. *Mmm!*

Cinnamon buns and fresh bread, plum pudding ... and then I recognised talcum powder and Pears soap.

Mum.

Shush, sang the sea trees, towering over me, cradling me almost. Every time I tried to step in a different direction, a sapling sprang up from the ground, shot up, blooming, before bending its branches, shushing and swaying.

Delicious comforting smells from my old life led the way, and I moved along with the trees' bowing branches. I knew I shouldn't follow them, but I couldn't stop. I had to know where they were leading me – who they were leading me to.

The swaying stopped. The trees parted and there she was. Right in front of me.

A tiny sensible part of me knew she wasn't real, and yet there was her long golden-brown hair tumbling down her back ... I breathed in her honeysuckle perfume, saw the crinkles from her laugh lines, the flour streaks from rolling out jam tarts dusted on her cheeks ... I could see her, feel her, hear her. I wanted this vision of Mum from when I was five to be true so badly.

I had never wanted anything more.

Come to me.

Whirling backwards, barefoot and smiling, she beckoned to me. No words were needed, because our bond was beyond language and reason, our hearts drawing back together, as one. As it always should have been.

I have been waiting for you.

We belonged to one another. I stretched out my arms, fingers tingling and tense, as I reached for my mother's hands ...

Look how beautiful you've become. My wonderful girl. I always knew you would be. You are more than enough.

I had nothing else to worry about – I only needed to let myself *be*, to drift back into the warmth of her love. I stepped towards her ...

Crack!

I ducked, covering my head, as wood splintered around me. The trees groaned and swung back, creating a space around me.

'Heather!' A boy's voice, a young voice, carried by the wind echoed through the trees. 'Come back!'

The vison of my mother faltered.

Perhaps ... there is a better time for us.
Her gentle voice chimed like bells in my mind. *I shall
come back for you. Another time, another place.*

The trees moved again, closing in around her and
blocking me out. I couldn't see through the thorny
branches. I didn't know how to get through. I couldn't
reach her.

She was gone. A*gain.*

'HEATHER!'

Lloyd?

His lips were moving, and he was sniffling and
shaking me hard by both arms, and somehow, I was
bleeding, my forearms and hands red and scratched.

'You'd gone into a maze. The trees kept moving,
closing tight around you, and we couldn't get to you.'
Lloyd tore off a strip from his shirt and wrapped it
carefully around my bleeding palms.

'You were fighting with the branches ... pulling
at them, and I don't know, but you were sobbing and
really giving them what for!'

'I heard Davey. He was calling to me.'

'That was just more tricks!' Nat said.

'I saw my mother,' I said, hardly recognising my own voice. 'I know it wasn't real, but I really wanted it to be.'

Lloyd nodded and touched my arm. 'I know,' he said. 'The Fae know how to hurt us. What we most want. They're powerful and it's hard to fight against.'

I looked at his agonised expression, and at Nat, shivering and wide-eyed. I glanced down at my scratched and bleeding arms. The Fae had almost got to me. If Lloyd hadn't searched for me, I might still be lost.

'We need to play some tricks of our own,' said Nat, taking an arrow from his quiver and stretching it across his bow.

'Where's Arlene?' I asked. 'Isn't she with you?'

Groaning, Lloyd clutched his head and rocked back and forth. 'We lost her in the maze. Everything happened so fast I couldn't even see her trace. We have to find her! Quickly now, before anything else happens. We *have to* stay together! We need to do better than this, or they're going to win!'

I nodded and checked my sword in its scabbard, ready to face whatever came next.

Enough of their lies! Pal spoke the truth. Even if the Champion had corrupted them over the years, the Fae had chosen to lie and manipulate. We had to stop them.

'Let's go and get Arlene back! Whatever tricks they pull next can't be worse than what they've already tried.'

Lloyd nodded. 'But be ready for anything and stay together.' He clasped Nat's shoulder. 'This way.'

* * *

Now that the trees had gone back to their original positions, we moved forwards, quickly coming to a narrow muddy path which opened on to a wide flat expanse. As we approached, we could see footprints around a vast lake, edged with thick black reeds.

'A lake,' I said.

'Exactly like the one up above in our world!' Lloyd exclaimed.

We stared out across the water. 'If this is the same, then we know where Fablehouse should be,' Lloyd added. 'Once we find Arlene we'll head there next. If we haven't seen anyone yet, then that must be where the Champion is holding everyone.'

This lake wasn't quite the same though. I missed the birds. Up above we'd spotted swallows and swifts and heard the cuckoo's call. Here it was silent, apart from the sound of the water softly lapping the bank. The black reeds were oily, densely packed and over two yards high. They swished around the outside of the lake, sounding like whispering.

I squinted. Was that . . . ? I nudged Lloyd. 'Is *that* Arlene?'

A long, shadowed figure stood on the other side of the lake, across from us, bending down over the water. But it couldn't be seen clearly, and you'd need a boat to cross to the other side.

'How did she get all the way over there?' I ran towards the water's edge. 'Arlene!'

But she didn't look up. *Squelch.* I looked down. My boot had sunk into black sludge which splurged up, quickly covering my boot. I bent round to Nat and Lloyd behind me. 'Don't come any further!'

'Why not?' Nat asked.

Gulch. The mud belched and bubbles of gas popped, forcing me down further, the bottom of my sword vanishing. 'The ground, the mud – it's sucking me in. I'm sinking!'

I *was being dragged under.*

'Quick – throw me a branch!' So far only my boots had gone completely under, but the mud guzzled at my skin, and my legs felt so heavy. Too heavy to lift.

I could feel myself being dragged down. Muddy reeds wrapped themselves around my calves, creeping upward.

'Hang on!' Lloyd yelled.

Nat lassoed a vine around his head, whipping it through the air. 'Catch this!'

I doubted it was tough enough to drag me out of this oily mulch, but as it came swinging towards me, I snatched at it.

'It'll break!' I panted, trying to grip it, my fingers already slimy.

'It's tough.' Nat grinned. 'Just like us! The Fae make us see whatever they want but we can trick *them.* Make this vine whatever you want – believe it will hold you!'

'Nat's right, H!' Lloyd shouted. 'Use your imagination!'

I tried, I really did; but I didn't see magic everywhere like Nat did. This was only a vine and would snap if I pulled too hard. Lloyd focused and Nat looked so eager, but I felt suddenly desperate. We *weren't* all together: Arlene wasn't with us. This wasn't a fight we could win. Tiredness enveloped me.

Would it really be so bad to give in and just stay here ... ?

Shoulders slumping, I let go and watched the vine slither down into the mud. *We'd tried.*

'Heather!' Nat cried. 'Grab it, we'll pull you out. Come on!'

I wanted to try but my eyes prickled hot with tears. Mud belched up my calves, sucking my knees down under. *Maybe it was time to stop struggling ...*

'We can do this!' Lloyd shouted. 'We've *chosen* to be heroes ... come on! Believe in yourself. Believe in us!'

The air around us darkened suddenly, as if storm clouds had rolled across the sky, although there was no sky here.

Rumbling vibrated around us, thundering through the soles of my feet. It reminded me of Pal's voice. The hairs on my arms prickled awake. *Pal!* Like a bright light, an image flashed into my mind, of him laughing by the lake, teaching us to duck and parry. Of when he told me he understood me, and how I could direct my anger . . .

I could feel it already roiling inside me like always. I closed my eyes and focused in on it, letting it build. I gritted my teeth and pushed against the mud drawing me downwards. I plunged my hand into the mud, scrabbling for the vine, and as I stretched to grab it, heat surged through my hands and fingers.

I looked ahead of me. Embers skittered across the surface of the mud and into the water. As they bounced like Nat's skimming stones had above, waves careened through the water and drew the embers underneath, deep into the lake. They didn't blink out; their light shone on, flickering fiercely as they sank to the depths.

The reeds around the edge shivered and then separated. From the middle of the lake appeared a coiled silver rope which unfurled like a fern. It spread out across the water and stopped, glittering right in front of me.

'Believe in us, Heather!' yelled Nat. 'Take it!'

Chapter Eighteen

The Lady of the Lake

I didn't need to be told twice. I snapped up the rope. It zigzagged through the water, pulling at me, until I was dragged back up on to the muddy, soggy bank. Panting, I let go of the rope and watched the water swallow it back up. I blinked and rubbed my eyes. *Had that really just happened?*

Nat threw his arms around me. We laughed in relief, me all muddy, when Nat's jaw fell open. I followed what he was gawping at. A tall, graceful lady with long dark hair appeared out of the middle of the lake.

She glided closer to us, as if skating on the surface of the lake. Her skin was honey-coloured, warm-green veins visible, and her turquoise eyes set wide apart. She examined us in turn, and her gaze stopped on me. Up above, our Lady of the Lake had gifted us our enchanted weapons, so was this someone we could trust? Even if she had sent the rope to help me, from what I'd seen of Fae Feld, I wasn't going to take any chances.

'Hello, children,' she said tenderly. 'I'm so glad to meet you at last.' Her voice illuminated the water around her, and dragonflies with iridescent bodies scattered. If her voice was a colour, it would have been sea-green. 'I am glad my rope was of assistance.'

'Who are you? Why did you help us?' I said frostily, my eyes narrowed. My hand tightened around my sword's hilt. I moved in front of the others, making sure they were away from the lake's edge in case she tried to drag us under.

She bowed her chin, her hair radiant and rippling, glossy shiny auburn. 'I have a proposition.' She dipped down into the water and ripples flowed outward. 'Your friend – the pretty one over there enchanted by her own reflection. I can bring her to you.'

She could bring Arlene back. Of course – she could swim to her. I scowled – it couldn't be that simple. I wasn't falling for any more Fae tricks! I gritted my teeth – *let her just try.*

Lloyd had the same thought as me. 'And what do we need to do in return?'

'Nothing.'

I almost laughed. 'Nothing?'

Her eyes widened. 'Well, perhaps indulge me for a while in further conversation? I'm lonely. It's been many moons since I have had the pleasure of human company.'

We looked at each other. *Was this another temptation, distraction?*

Nat tugged on my sleeve. 'We need Arlene!'

Lloyd looked at me pointedly. We *did* need Arlene. How could we rescue the others if we lost her?

'OK, we agree,' I said. 'But just bring her to us. Nothing else, no funny business!'

She smiled with dimples in her cheeks. The water droplets shivered on her skin like droplets of glass as she sank under the water, not a ripple to be seen. We scanned the surface of the lake, but it was as if she'd never appeared at all. Before I could say anything, the water parted and she rose next to us, carrying a magically dry and smiling Arlene in her arms.

'Arlene!'

She set Arlene gently down at the water's edge, shuddering slightly as her hand touched dry land. I rushed over to Arlene, helping her to sit up. She set down her axe and didn't look at any of us. The look on her face was faraway and dreamy.

'What's the matter with her?' Nat asked me, concerned.

I frowned. 'I don't know!'

'She is temporarily mesmerised,' the woman said. 'The Fae magic will wear off in a moment or two. Allow her some breathing space.'

We sat down on the bank next to Arlene. Lloyd cleared his throat and I looked at him. He raised his eyebrows, nodding towards the woman.

'We have somewhere to be,' I said firmly. 'So if you want your ... conversation, I say, best get to it. If you aren't part of the Fae, then who are you?'

She smiled at each of us.

'I only wish to offer you comfort. I understand you've been let down, and deeply hurt.' Her words settled over us as we registered what she was saying. 'I understand. I too am like you.' Her smile was sad. She swept her long hair round to one side and started absently plaiting it, her long fingers nimble.

But she hadn't answered my question.

'Who are you?' Nat gazed at her with his mouth open.

'I'm an outcast. Unwanted in the world above and so banished here many realms ago. Shunned and reviled for nothing more than being born into this skin that I'm in. The Fae hate us humans. And they hate those of us who are different even more so.'

'Why?' I asked.

'Because we have *true* power. We know that power isn't about control, but about knowledge and kindness. They believe that by making us afraid, we'll shrink. They think we can be tamed and kept small. That we'll go away, shrivel up, ashamed.'

I glanced at Arlene, still dazed. This woman had helped us, she had rescued Arlene, but there was something about her I didn't quite trust. Perhaps I just didn't trust anything in this dank, dim light. Shadows and secrets surrounded us; the air was deep with them. What spells was she trying to weave?

'I'm not ashamed!' I said firmly.

She looked at me approvingly and nodded. 'Thank goodness that flame inside you burns bright, my girl! I feel your righteous anger. You are entitled to it. Make sure it scorches anyone who comes too close. Raze your enemies to the ground. Don't let them fool you into believing you are powerless, for you have strength within that they cannot begin to imagine!'

Lloyd and I shared a look. His voice threaded through my mind. We knew advice didn't come for free; what were we being made to believe here? What weren't we seeing?

'I will tell you what the future looks like for children like you. It is bleak. You will be always kept on the outside. On the fringes. Why contribute to a society which treats you so unfairly? You owe them nothing. You are all special, far too good for the human realm. Your veins contain the *true* you, such value you carry inside. Stay here and I will help you discover and harness it.'

'Help us how?' asked Lloyd.

'I can help you become anything you want to be by unleashing your true power on to the world,' the woman replied, plucking a grey lily from the reeds, and threading it through her long plait. 'I mean you no harm. In fact, I will prove it. See – you, girl ... you are bleeding. You are hurt. I can make all your hurt go away.'

Her voice was a warm blanket on a cold night, a foot rub after you'd been walking all day ... She moved swiftly, seamlessly silent, through the water, suddenly in front of us.

She laid her hands on my arms and we all watched, astonished, as the blood from my scratches dried up and the broken skin knotted over. 'All better – look!'

Nat, Lloyd and I stared at her. *She healed me.* She didn't have to do that. But again, something felt wrong. I couldn't work out why she wanted to help us. What was in it for her?

Arlene still looked glassy-eyed, but she couldn't take her eyes off the woman in the lake.

'I was trapped here, many years ago. At first, I

believed I'd never get over it. I never stopped struggling, trying to escape, but … I came to realise that there is grace in acceptance. And being here has been the making of me. You are welcome to stay, you would be under my guidance and protection.'

'But if we stayed, how could we help the others trapped down here?' I asked. 'It's one thing *choosing* to be here, but another to be taken and held against your will.'

'Please – help us?' Lloyd could barely look at her, fingers awkwardly clenching and unclenching at his side. 'We have to find the taken ones! Do you know where they are? Do you know how we can defeat the Champion?'

'The Fae do not include me in their plans. But I know the Champion's fortress lies that way.' She pointed towards the direction Fablehouse would be up above in our world. 'I cannot offer you much guidance other than to say the Champion is boastful. He is full of himself and his schemes. His overconfidence may be his downfall. He doesn't expect anyone to challenge him – perhaps you could use that to your advantage.' She drifted back, deeper into the lake.

'Will you come with us?' Nat asked.

She shook her head, dark hair sticking to her cheeks. 'I'm afraid I cannot. I'm not permitted to leave this lake.' Her slender fingers stroked the water. 'One day though, I hope to be strong enough to be land bound. To wander freely in the world...'

'Can we help *you*?' Nat's lips wobbled. He didn't want to leave her here, I could tell.

Her smile was forlorn. 'No one can help me, yet. Only a great change to the order of this world will free me. For now, I wish you good luck and good health. When you are ready, call for me. Who knows, perhaps I'll even visit you in your dreams. Together we can reach your potential and achieve glorious things!'

Nat walked towards her, ankle-deep into the lake, stretching out his hands. The woman extended her own arms towards his and wisps of purple echoed off her fingertips, before she disappeared back into the rustling reeds which closed around her, swallowing her up.

'What?' Nat blinked and started splashing at the water. 'Where did she go?'

From the swaying black reeds, we heard, 'Come back soon, my children!' very faintly.

Arlene raised her hand and rubbed her face. Her eyes began to clear, as if she were waking from a long dream. 'See you soon!' she murmured, waving her fingers.

'Arlene – are you all right?' I asked urgently. 'What did the Fae show you?'

Shivering, she pulled her legs up and wrapped her arms around her knees. 'She looked like those Hollywood movie stars on Lloyd's cigarette cards.' Arlene rested her head on her arms. 'So glamorous.'

We stared at the silent, dark lake for a long while. There were no glowing, glassy eyes, or tendrils of smoky Fae. For the first time since we'd entered Fae Feld, it didn't feel like we were being watched. We were completely alone.

'Now what?' I said.

'We go to Fablehouse,' Lloyd said. 'Or whatever passes for it down here. Everyone must be there. We don't just give up on them.'

Chapter Nineteen

Captive

Leaving the lake, Lloyd suddenly stopped and pointed just ahead of us.

'Look there – movement.' Dirt and earth had been all churned up. Squinting in both directions, he got on his hands and knees, staring at the ground. 'Here, maybe . . .' He raked his fingers through the mulch.

Nat and Lloyd led the way. Arlene and I walked slower, behind. I kept sneaking glances at her.

'What did the Fae tempt you with?' I asked. 'Why haven't you said nothin'? Arlene!'

'It wasn't anything like that.' She wrinkled her nose. She'd lost her dazed look, but still had a strange smile, and she kept drifting off, mid-sentence. 'I wasn't . . . *tempted*.'

'What are you talking about? You were all gaga at the lake – you didn't even see us there!'

'It was more like . . .' She sighed. 'It was more like I was shown something, in the water. Patterns . . . of how things *could be* . . .'

'Like what?'

She shook her head. 'You wouldn't understand—'

'There!' Lloyd hissed.

Twenty feet ahead stood the remains of an ancient castle, now just decaying ruins. Crumbling thick structures of stone turrets stained green with moss and mildew. Rusting chains splayed on the ground. The remains of a drawbridge with splintered planks, but no moat, only a dip in the ground where it had dried up.

Behind a row of trees, I sidled next to Lloyd and pointed, keeping my voice low.

'Can you see what I—'

'The children? Yes,' he replied, his eyes searching.

Sitting on stone benches in rows, as if listening to lessons, with their backs to us, facing the biggest, most complete structure – a tower – were all the children from Fablehouse: Martha, Leon, Henry, Michael, Judy, Jeremiah, Carole, Ruth and Davey. I nearly cried out seeing little Davey's mop. I'd recognise him anywhere. But while he wasn't like the changeling I had seen in the common room, he wasn't quite himself either. Sitting still with a straight back, for one thing.

'Davey . . .' My voice clogged with tears.

'I think they're under a Fae spell.' Arlene nudged me. 'But that's only the children. Where's Miss Gloria and Cook and the other grown-ups?'

I had no idea. I couldn't see any adults. Stood behind the children were nine imposing figures, one for each child. From behind, we could see they were tall, much taller than any adult, and clad head to toe in grey metal armour that clanged when they moved. Each of them held a thick wooden staff studded with faded coloured stones.

'Who *are* they?' Nat pointed at them. 'Fae guards?'

Lloyd turned to me. 'What do you think, H?'

'I think the Fae can look as different as we do. Yep, these must be soldiers or guards.'

'Not the good guys, that's for sure!' Arlene said.

As one of them turned around, I nearly yelped, seeing a rectangular eye slit in a pointy helmet that covered the rest of their face. A dull yellow glint came from it. I clutched Lloyd's sleeve, and Nat and Arlene hunched closer to us.

'That's our lot.' Lloyd rubbed his forehead. 'But how do we get them back, H?'

How could we fight these guards? They were huge and had armour!

'I could try and confuse them,' Nat suggested. 'Create a distraction?'

Lloyd and I both said, 'How?'

'By doing some magic tricks.' Nat turned out his pockets and showed us juggling balls, a length of rope and a pack of playing cards. 'I always come prepared.' He grinned. 'If they can make *us* see stuff that ain't really there, then maybe if I believe hard enough – I can do the same to them!'

'And if it doesn't work, then we could go back to that nice lady for help?' Arlene suggested.

'Good thinking, Arlene,' Lloyd said, smiling at her.

What? How was that a good thing?

Anger sizzled inside me – why did Lloyd always

rely on grown-ups? And Arlene – why did she suddenly trust anyone down here?

'That woman can't leave the lake, and we're not going back,' I spat.

Lloyd recoiled. 'It was just a thought, H.'

'A bad one,' I grumbled. 'It's just us, remember that!'

'OK . . . I'm going in,' Nat said bravely. 'Wish me luck!'

Arlene patted him on the back. 'You don't need luck,' she whispered. 'You have talent!'

Nat beamed at her before jogging forward across the hilly mound. He ran out directly in front of the children and the guards, juggling as he went. 'Your entertainment has arrived!'

The guards turned to one another, confused. Hissing, they hunched low over the children they stood behind, ready to attack at any moment.

'Your master sent me!' Nat crowed, so confidently that their hissing died down.

'This'd better work,' Lloyd murmured. Arlene crossed her fingers. I peeked out from behind the tree. The guards were transfixed on the balls Nat was effortlessly tossing into the air. It *was* working.

'*Cripes!*' Lloyd gasped, pointing at the balls.

Arlene's mouth hung open too. As the balls left Nat's hands, they changed from being solid objects into luminous see-through globes filled with coloured liquid – cherry-red, primrose-yellow, sky-blue – the liquid inside sloshing about. Nat's hands weren't anywhere near them! And then the balls transformed, changing into different shapes. The liquid inside frothed and sputtered, throwing up flecks of gold.

'How's he *doing* that?' Arlene said, turning to us, amazed.

I laughed. 'Nat was right. He has magic of his own!'

Lloyd beamed at me. 'He certainly does!'

We just needed to believe.

'He must have *really* practised!' Arlene giggled.

'I *think* . . . maybe he's . . .' I swallowed. 'Nat's *really* magic now.'

'There's something about being here, in Fae Feld,' Lloyd said. 'I feel different too.'

Hope and excitement rushed into my chest. Maybe we *could* do this. Maybe we *were* special enough!

'It's his true power – the way he can transform anything!'

The guards stared at the balls in awe, and then began excitedly whispering to one another in fast, high-pitched tones. One by one they bounced up and down. Something like laughter came from them, as they clapped their hands together, unable to stop staring at the colours spinning through the air.

More . . . the air buzzed. *We want more!*

Inside the balls there now appeared shiny gold coins and big jewels, showing the guards riches beyond their wildest dreams. They snapped their fingers and swiped at the balls, trying to capture them.

Mine! A guard rushed forward, hoping to touch the glowing orbs, transfixed. Two guards clanged helmets jumping up at the same time. The sound clanged loudly through the air.

Watching Nat juggle, we knew he had tapped into his own brand of magic, just like Lloyd had managed to do with his tracking ability. I thought of the sparks I'd created at the lake and when I'd tried to wake Lloyd from his trance. Was that my magic? And what power might Arlene have?

'Let's move,' Lloyd said. We crept around the

guards, who were still staring up at the traces of colour and light swirling in the air.

Emerging from the trees came the adults from Fablehouse: Miss Gloria, Miss Betty and Miss Clara, and Cook. But no Miss Isolde. They trudged on the spot with no expression, their bare, bleeding feet in the dirt.

Me, Lloyd and Arlene ran between them, shaking their arms and waving our hands in front of their eyes, but they were bewitched just like the children, and had no idea who we were. No wonder the guards could stop to watch Nat's performance.

I ran over to the children. 'We'll get you out of here,' I whispered to little Davey, crouching in front of the stone bench, but his eyes were blank too. He gave no sign that he'd even heard me. 'Follow us.'

'Come on!' Lloyd said, taking Judy's hand, but then just as quickly he let it go. 'She's ice cold!' Judy didn't look at him.

'Lloyd, I don't think they can hear us!' My voice rose. 'But look … I think somehow they still recognise Miss Gloria.'

The children stood up at the same time and streamed towards Miss Gloria.

Arlene sniffed. 'I hate seeing the tinies like this!' Her eyes filled with tears. 'They look so empty . . .' She put her arm round Judy's shoulder and began singing 'Somewhere Over the Rainbow', a tune Judy used to ask her to sing all the time.

Arlene's voice was always lovely, but now, here, in this place, it truly soared. I'd never heard anything else like it. Every time a note faded, a chime sounded. As the notes rocketed through the air, the grass under our feet squirmed, as if it were dancing,

Life flickered in Judy's eyes, and she turned her head towards Arlene. She blinked slowly.

'I think –' Arlene gasped, turning to us – 'she can hear me, and my singing!'

Judy flashed her a shy smile. Other children stopped on their way to Miss Gloria, swivelling their heads in the direction of Arlene's voice.

'Stop singing for a moment,' I said. 'Just to see if anything changes.'

As Arlene's last note died away, Judy's eyes deadened, as if a candle had been blown out, and she stepped backwards, away from Arlene, arms rigid at her sides.

'Keep singing!' Lloyd and I nudged each other. 'Arlene! Your singing *is* actually magic!' Lloyd exclaimed. 'Look, they're waking up!'

And they were! Davey started smiling; Martha, Carole and Ruth's faces softened and lifted upwards. I could hardly believe it, but Arlene's voice was reaching a part of them that the Fae couldn't get to.

Leon and Michael began drumming their fingers on their legs, and Henry's and Michael's toes started tapping. Arlene's song bounded off every tree and bush, sprang off the collapsing castle walls. Closed ferns began to flare open.

'Remember, Arlene, you're the star of the show, all right? You can do this!' I said, patting her arm. 'Now, walk off and see if they follow.'

Lloyd came next to me. 'Whatever you do – keep on singing!'

'Nat! You can stop now,' I yelled. 'Follow Arlene.'

Arlene moved away, her beautiful voice threading through the trees, and, just like the Pied Piper, everyone followed, drawn by her serenading.

Nat's juggling balls landed at his feet. As they hit the ground, they split, splashing coloured liquid. The guards watched the sparkling liquid seep into the earth, leaving pinpricks of gold. They fell to their knees, frantically raking through the mud, trying to collect whatever riches they could.

'Lead them all to the cairn entrance!' I called after Arlene and Nat. 'And hurry!'

'H and me will head into the ruins of the tower,' Lloyd added. 'We'll find Miss Isolde. If it's safe, come back and help us when you've handed everyone over to Pal.'

I watched Arlene and Nat as they vanished over the hill, hoping their singing and illusions would protect them from further Fae tricks. They'd be all right; they were together.

'Got your sword ready?' Lloyd asked.

I drew my sword and aimed it in front of me as the guards now stared at their empty hands: no jewels or riches to be found. They scowled and grunted, glaring at us accusingly. Spitting and realising the children had gone, they dashed their helmets to the ground and surrounded us.

Now it was just Lloyd and me and a bunch of angry guards. We moved back to back.

Even with their helmets off, it was impossible to tell if the guards were men or women. Their lashless eyes were the colour of mustard, and their cheeks sunken and hollow. Their noses were stubby but fleshy, with one giant nostril, instead of two. Their grins were wide and toothless, with thin and almost grey lips.

'What should we do?' I shouted to Lloyd over my shoulder.

'Try speaking to them, H!'

What? What use was talking?

But then I remembered the words I'd said to the Fae when they'd bewitched Lloyd, and how a fiery glow had surrounded and protected us.

What if I told them the truth?

I closed my eyes, even though the guards approached, aiming their gnarled staffs at us. I cowered, feeling small, but opened my mouth anyway and tried to let my instincts lead me.

'Please, listen to what I have to say.' I stared at each of them in turn; seeing them for who they really were. They stopped moving and glanced at one another, huddled together.

'We haven't come to hurt you. We're not trying to take your home, this land, or anything that belongs to you.'

They turned to one another, heads half cocked, listening. Noise burbled up as they began talking amongst themselves.

'You have been lied to. You don't have to do what you're told, just because your fathers and mothers and grandparents might have done. You have your own lives and it's up to you how you choose to lead them. You *must* think for yourselves.'

Voices overlapped, tones of disagreement coming forward.

We serve the Champion, came a chorus. *It is in our blood. He has promised us riches; we will be rewarded once all the humans above have been replaced. Then our reign begins, we will witness a new dawn, and we will be free.*

I jumped on to a nearby boulder and raised my sword, showing them that I meant business. 'But there are more valuable things than riches! Riches won't change your fortune. Our friends don't belong to you! You can't *steal* people. Even if the Champion stole your lives, replacing all the humans won't lead you to freedom. It will only keep you longer in the darkness.'

They stared at me and their murmurs grew louder, their tones urgent. Ancient distant languages rumbled across the valleys. *Lies, lies, lies . . .*

'So where *are* these riches then?' I asked. 'How long have you been kept waiting? I'm from the mortal realm, and I can tell you the streets are not paved with gold. There is suffering there too. You have nothing to gain by taking over the human realm. You need to find your own way to live.'

We listen only to the Champion! a voice hollered. Fists pummelled armour. It clanged. *He has ruled this realm for eons. Enough of your trickery!*

Why wouldn't they listen? The lot of them had been brainwashed.

'You're the ones being tricked! Can't you see that? This is your world. Why do you let someone else boss you round? What was it like before he came? Can you even remember?'

The air seemed to stop – the rustling leaves and slithering vines quietened.

'Isn't this *your* land?' I shouted into the silence.

'They're really listening, H,' Lloyd whispered, now by my side. 'Can you feel it?'

And I really could. All the eyes peeking out from bushes and trees that had been tracking us since we'd arrived were focused on us. Everyone in Fae Feld was listening to me.

'You don't need to blindly follow any more. Faith doesn't come from fear. There's an army of you. Strength and power come when you work together. Instead of serving one master, perhaps now it's time to serve yourselves. Change can begin at any time, and can begin with you.'

Claim what is ours . . . stronger together . . . united we fight . . .

Lloyd offered me his hand and I took it, jumping down off the boulder. I thrust my sword back into its scabbard.

'Let it be known that the Roamers are here!' Lloyd said, as our linked hands shot into the air. 'We are here to claim back what's ours. And now is the time for you to do the same.'

The Fae guards bowed their heads a little

and moved to the side. One of them swept their arm along the ground, right through the middle of their circle.

'Lloyd. They're letting us pass.'

As I glimpsed their faces, no longer bunched into tight scowls, my shoulders relaxed. Their eyes seemed brighter somehow – more alive with the energy of belief returned to them.

Lloyd and I gave each other a relieved smile. I was glad that we didn't need to fight the guards, but I knew we'd have to face their master, this Champion. One battle down, one to go. And this was a fight we couldn't afford to lose.

Chapter Twenty

The Champion

The silence surrounding us was eerie, but there was a feeling of peace in the air too, of something being settled or decided.

The ruins of the ancient castle lay before us. A few stone structures and forts. We headed towards a tall stone archway that lay beyond a steep path. Thick shrubs shifted in the ground, allowing us through. Overgrown plants no longer tangled themselves round our feet.

'Can you see much?' I asked. 'Of Miss Isolde?'

'Yes, her trace is strong. This way!'

Perfume threaded through the air, not the rich

heaviness of before, but something light, like lilies. We walked towards the archway, kicking aside piles of rusted chains as we passed them.

'There!' I pointed ahead, through the archway, where, next to a splintered tree trunk, Miss Isolde stared up intently at an imposing figure, clad head to toe in glossy bronze armour. He moved slowly through a series of movements, like a ritual.

'Lloyd, is that the Champion?' I whispered. 'He's huge.'

We inched forward. This had to be him. Mark, the so-called leader of the Fae, the friend who had betrayed Pal, abandoning him to fight the Questing Beast alone.

As the Champion moved through his routine, and we moved even closer, we baulked. He was the height of three men, and twice as wide. Bearded, he towered over Miss Isolde. His copper breastplate shone, the metal glinting. Wrapped around his forearms were vines and leaves which pulsed as he moved, their purple veins glistening.

'Please . . .' Miss Isolde begged, her voice cracked. 'Please, stop all this.' She buried her face in her hands and wept quietly. My heart squashed tight, and it was all I could do not to rush forward and comfort her.

'Is this not what you wanted?' the Champion bellowed, but unlike Pal's smooth rounded tones, he sounded edgy, the words harsh and tight. 'For everyone to forget you existed?' he boomed.

Miss Isolde shook her head. Her hair was no longer up in a bun, but now wild and loose around her shoulders, with streaks of silver, white and grey threaded through it. 'Not like this! This is evil.'

The Champion laughed. 'You human creatures are such fools. Good and evil do not exist. All that matters are words and actions: what you say and what you do. You called all of this into existence by your desire!'

What did he mean? I frowned at Lloyd.

'But I made a mistake!' she cried. 'I thought I was protecting them! My loyalty is to the children and our land.'

The Champion warrior sneered. 'Loyalty? My lady, it is too late for that.' He bent, armour clanging, and peered into her eyes. 'The grimoire was found in your possession. *You* began meddling and making deals. We have kept our part of the bargain and hidden you away, as you asked.'

'No ... no ... The book, it – tricked me!' She flinched from his mouth, only inches from hers, turning her head away. 'I didn't know what the book was ... or that it held such power.'

'You tell yourself falsehoods, my lady. You wanted to relinquish control. Give yourself over to a wilder power.'

The Champion circled her, taunting. 'You spoke the words at the cairn. You opened the doorway and invited us in. *You* wanted these troublesome children off your hands, out of the way.'

I gasped. Was he speaking the truth? That this – all of this – was Miss Isolde's fault?

'Your dreams and every thought were filled with putting Fablehouse under a veil.' He spat this last word, full of disgust. 'Thinking you could protect those who lived within.'

There was a sharp intake of breath from Miss Isolde. 'I didn't realise you'd trick me by replacing us and bringing us here!' Her tears splashed on to the mud. 'I wish I'd never found that book. I've failed those children.'

'We both know no one cares about these abandoned children. No one is coming to save them, or you. You should make peace with this being your new home.'

He raised his arms, and a dark green mist churned around his head. 'Soon changelings will be in every home in the country. My dominion begins in this tiny village, but soon my Fae army shall march on the world!'

I looked at Lloyd, who reached for my hand. With every word this man uttered, it felt as if I were being struck. How dare he think he could take over Fablehouse because no one cared? He *had no idea.*

My blood boiled, the fury inside me heating up and pulsing through my veins. I felt it, like an electric charge.

He hadn't counted on the Roamers. He hadn't counted on me!

'The changelings lie in wait in the village. The replacement of loved ones has already begun. Soon, every hamlet, every town and city, will have a changeling at their hearth.'

'If his army advances, we're done for!' I said. 'Lloyd, what can we do?'

'Let's show him who we are.' Lloyd squared his shoulders, determined. 'The book said only the Chosen can defeat him. Let's say *we're* the Chosen. Unsettle him. Make him think we're to be reckoned with.'

I nodded. Fablehouse would never be safe unless this Champion was beaten. The Lady of the Lake had said he wouldn't expect a challenge. We had to get Miss Isolde away from him. I just hoped Nat and Arlene already had the others safe.

What had Nat said about illusions? *Believe them and they could be true.* Would the Champion believe we were the Chosen? Even just for a moment? There was only one way to find out.

I wasn't going to run. Not this time. Some things were worth fighting for. I'd stand here and fight with my friend. We'd fight for each other, for Pal, and for Fablehouse.

Our home.

Chapter Twenty-One

The Battle

I stepped forward, feet firmly planted with my sword raised.

'Heather! Lloyd!' cried Miss Isolde, staring at us. 'How ... What are you doing here?'

Before we could reply, the Champion roared. 'What feeble folk are these?' He glared at us and stepped in front of Miss Isolde.

'We are the Chosen – here to do battle!' I announced, making my voice low and commanding. I gripped my sword tightly to stop my hands from shaking; the anger swirled up and down my arms, warming the blade.

The Champion spun around. Staring at Lloyd's spear and my sword, he burst into deep, sarcastic laughter.

'You two? Chosen? Despite your trinkets – I think not.'

He raised his arms above his head, and a tree stump, next to me, began quaking in the ground. The Champion stared at it, squashing his hands into fists, and it wrenched right out of the ground, tearing through the air.

What chance did we have against this?

'We said: we are the Chosen!' Lloyd shouted.

I felt a crush of pressure grip my stomach and chest, but it wasn't painful. I glanced down. My pinafore jolted, and out of nowhere silver chainmail appeared, flickering like the silvery scales on a fish. They covered my clothes, shielding me and protecting my arms and legs. And the same was happening to Lloyd!

'What's happening?' Lloyd gasped, staring down at himself.

Clunk! Clang!

Moving, I noticed that the armour wasn't heavy at

all; if anything, it had moulded itself to my body, and I felt light and nimble.

Even though I didn't understand how this was possible, I flashed Lloyd a smile. 'We're *real* knights now!'

Lloyd leaped up, his spear held aloft as if about to do some damage. He glared at the Champion. 'And why can't we be Chosen?' he challenged.

Towering over us, the Champion stroked his beard, eyes steely like chips of flint. 'Chosen don't look like you.'

'What *do* they look like then?' Lloyd said, standing tall and straight. He slammed his spear into the ground, and tremors thudded through my body. The anger rose in my throat now, my eyes burning as I narrowed them.

'The Chosen are of regal birth. You cannot lay claim to the position.' The Champion curled his lip, spitting on the ground. 'Look at the state of you! Ragtag weaklings. Children are no match for a great warrior like me.'

He banged his fists against his breastplate. The booms echoed through the air, causing the ground under our feet to shake.

'Pathetic!' he jeered. 'How dare you face me, a Champion, with your little toys! Call that a sword? Playtime is over! Even if you were fair of heart, you are not fair of . . . *skin*. Your claims remind me of a knight I once knew. Palamedes. Another pathetic knight who wasn't up to the task.'

At the mention of Pal's name, we stiffened. *Pal.* Our Pal. How dare this man taunt our friend?

'Palamedes also thought he could be a hero, once upon a time. Deluded fool. He never realised we only gave him the foolsome quests no one else wanted. He agreed to fight the Questing Beast, so desperate to be liked and accepted – to be one of us . . .' The Champion doubled over, hooting, almost wiping tears from his eyes. 'I escaped down here, knowing it was the perfect place to settle. He thought Merlin would be pleased that he tried to slay the Beast . . . but heroes do not look like him!'

His laughter rang out hollowly through the trees.

'Pal's worth a bloody million of you!' I screamed, spitting at him. 'You hid down here and left him to fight the Beast alone. Coward!'

The Champion growled and lunged forward. His

heavy footsteps thundered. 'I am the Champion! This is my land. Soon I will take your realm too. This is a war you *will not* win!'

'Pal is more warrior than you'll ever be!' Lloyd threw his spear, which narrowly missed the Champion charging towards him.

I remembered Miss Isolde telling us about the soldiers who'd fought for us, and I thought about our fathers, and the other men who'd died trying to make a united world. If that wasn't noble or regal, then what was?

I roared as Lloyd raced forwards.

He tried to jump on to the Champion's back, but he threw Lloyd off in a fury, knocking him to the ground. Lloyd rolled and moaned, clutching his side. No blood, but he couldn't catch his breath.

'You want a war – we'll give you a war!' I jumped forward in front of Lloyd, my sword aimed at the Champion's throat. 'We are the Chosen and we will defeat you!'

'You will never defeat me!' The Champion spun away from me, clapping his hands together. 'I command the land!' He hunkered down low. Stones and pebbles jerked and writhed on the ground. He flung his palm outwards, and the stones hurtled through the air. I ducked, sword ready to deflect them, in case they came my way.

Leaves on bushes shivered and fell to the ground. They slithered towards my feet, creeping over my boots. Hundreds of gleaming green eyes peered out from the undergrowth. The Fae guards! A low chanting began, reminding me of the deep drum I'd heard earlier. I strained to hear the words, but it wasn't in any language I recognised, though it fell in time to the beating of my heart, driving me forwards.

In front of me, the leaves all knitted together into one huge circular shield. I reached for it, my hand sliding effortlessly into the vine strap at the back. I held it up in front of my face. *The Fae were helping me?*

The bushes crunched, the leaves parted, and the Champion hollered, '*Stay!* I do not need your help to destroy these tiny humans, but watch me – observe and learn how I make light work of them. Notice how easy it is – they are nothing! This is how we will take the above!'

Next to me, Lloyd lifted himself off the ground,

every movement clearly painful. Staggering next to me, he breathed, 'Get him now. I see a weak spot ... above his breastplate. Aim there!'

I looked at where Lloyd was pointing, and even though I couldn't see the trace that he could, I steadied myself and pulled my arm back, feeling the tremble of effort as I tried to hold the sword firm.

As the Champion turned back to face us, I put everything I had into the throw and hurled my sword as hard as I could, feeling a weightlessness as I released it.

I stumbled forward ... It felt like time slowed and I watched the blade flying through the air, propelled by speed itself, arcing over and away from me. Sparks flowed from my fingertips, and they glanced off the shiny steel, making the Champion shield his eyes.

'Whoo!' Lloyd yelped as the sword's hilt struck the Champion right in the middle of his chest – *clang!*

Pride flared in my chest. Had we defeated him? The tip of the blade arched upwards and pierced his shoulder, causing him to stagger backwards.

'You've done it, H!'

The Champion snarled. 'Is that it?' He clutched his shoulder and scowled at the sword still lodged there. Wrestling the blade out, he snapped the sword in half, and tossed it behind him, sneering.

It was broken in two! *Now what?*

'Ludicrous!' he bellowed. 'Is that the best you can do?'

We had to try harder; to fight smarter. What else could we do? I looked at Lloyd, recovered now and poised in a fighting stance. We couldn't beat him – we needed Arlene and Nat. Only the Roamers all together could win this fight! Was there a weakness there, in his idea of himself? He had his arrogance . . .

'We're still standing, aren't we?' I ventured. 'We're going to beat you. How do you think we even got through here? Your guards let us pass. Your hold over them, and their land, is weakening.'

'Nothing about me is weak!' He beat a fist to his chest. 'Who cares if you have turned a couple of guards' heads? They mean nothing to me! Greedy little wretches, seduced by promises of gold! I only use them to do my bidding. They are worthless.'

He stared at me, hands on his hips, and I thought

of everyone who'd ever underestimated me. How dare he treat people like this! No one was worthless. Even the Fae. Fury gushed through me again, forming a tense, sizzling ball in my stomach. I *could use my anger . . . if I focused.*

Closing my eyes, I imagined my rage streaming down my arms as if it were lava from a volcano. Heat sputtered through my veins, smoke and flickers coming from my fingertips. From behind the Champion, I watched my broken sword flare red-hot; blazing as if being re-forged in a furnace. My eyes widened as the blade pulsed, orangey-red sparking along the sides.

I dived forward on to my stomach and slid through the Champion's legs. The earth churned up under me as my cheek scraped against the ground. The two sword halves dragged along the ground towards me, slamming together like magnets, clanging and glowing. The noise rang out like bells across the hillside. I flung myself at my sword's handle, picking it up effortlessly, the sword lighter than air.

As the Champion bent to grab me, Lloyd snatched up his spear from behind Mark and charged towards him. The spear spun and twirled through the air as Lloyd thrust and dodged, the stone flint jabbing the Champion's calves, as he swiftly sidestepped his thick swinging arms.

I sprang to my feet and swiped my sword through the air. The blade pierced the cloth jersey the champion wore under his breastplate as I dragged it down his side.

'You!' He winced as he gripped his torso. He spread his fingertips, recoiling at the blood seeping through. 'You dare draw blood from me?' he howled.

I whipped around backwards, feeling the fire continuing to flood every part of me, lighting me up from inside, my feet magically knowing exactly where to tread away from his grasping fingers.

Lloyd nimbly managed to evade the Champion. He was strong, but so heavy that he moved slowly; Lloyd practically pivoted around him.

'Stay still!' the Champion roared, frustrated, as he smashed into a tree trunk, rubbing his head and missing Lloyd by a mile.

'I can tell where he's going to go!' Lloyd crowed, springy on his feet as he darted this way and that, using his spear to deflect the Champion's mighty fists.

We were young and quick and kept on moving. He was no match for us! We were winning!

But suddenly the Champion leaped to the side and seized Lloyd, wrapping his thick arm around his neck, and pulling him close.

'Halt!' the Champion demanded. 'Stop your nonsense or else I will destroy him!'

The Champion curled his massive fingers and lifted Lloyd up off the ground, his legs frantically dangling in the air. The Champion had him.

Gulping, I froze. What could I do? This was all for nothing if I didn't have Lloyd at the end of it. Without Lloyd, there was nothing. What would I say to Nat and Arlene? The Roamers didn't exist without him. I dropped my sword, the clang dull as it hit the ground.

He shook Lloyd back and forth as if he were one of Judy's rag dolls. Watching the Champion's fingers tighten around Lloyd's neck, I fell on my knees, all hope deserting me.

Lloyd, no!

Lloyd gurgled and croaked, but I couldn't make

out any words. His eyes bulged. I panted, unable to take a breath as my heart seized. I covered my eyes, unable to watch.

But then a melody, out of nowhere, rocketed through the air. *Arlene?* Singing, strong and sure. *Arlene and Nat!*

The Champion whirled round in disbelief, dropping Lloyd, who crumpled into a heap. He put his hands over his ears, snarling, 'What is that unholy sound?'

As the song drew closer, the drumming started up again, the ground vibrating under my knees, the soft earth giving way. My tears soaked into the ground, turning the pale, dry mud dark.

Then I saw them come out through the ruins. They ran towards me. 'Pal's got 'em all!' Nat cried out. 'Everyone's safe!'

'Help! Lloyd and I gave it everything but it isn't enough. You're right, Nat, if we believe, we can make magic! But we have to do it together – it has to come from all of us. Arlene!' I shouted. 'Sing louder!'

Arlene sang and Nat's arrows flew through the air – *pew, pew, pew* – one after another, but the

Champion batted them away as easily as paper aeroplanes.

'Come on!' I yelled to them. 'We can beat him ... we've chosen to be the Chosen. It's about what we choose to believe and I *choose us*!'

I moved to protect Lloyd and draw him back closer to us. He started to stir and gather himself.

Arlene's powerful voice shook the leaves from the trees. They rained down, some as big as bed-sheets, and Nat moved his hands around, as if shaping clay, and they flew around the Champion's head, wrapping themselves around his face, slapping at his cheeks.

The ground throbbed under the Champion's feet, and his footing became unsteady.

'You'll never win!' My voice was hoarse now, but I didn't stop. He had to hear from the Roamers. 'Friendship is a magic that you'll never understand!'

It was now or never. I had to fight to save my friends, to save us all. Diving for my sword, I held it high before plunging it hard into the Champion's foot.

Yelping in agony, he dropped to his knees. With one hand he clutched his bleeding foot, the sword pulsing red-hot, and with the other he angrily swiped at the leaves covering his face.

'Guards!'

Noise around us swelled, but no guards came forth. Why would they, now they'd seen the truth? They knew what he really thought of them. Their chanting started up again, words we didn't understand, but that now struck me as magnificent, in its own way, as Arlene's singing.

The four of us gathered around the Champion writhing on the ground, hands over his ears. Arlene leaned over him, singing, the pitch steadily increasing.

'Stop!' he whined pitifully. 'It hurts!'

'The truth does,' I replied. 'And *your* truth is that you're weak, not strong. You're a bully and a coward, and now *everyone* knows it!'

Like flickering flames, the eyes hidden in the bushes all blinked shut and droves of Fae guards came to stand in front of the ruins. They opened their mouths, and their chanting became bolder and louder.

'What are they saying?' Nat called, over the din.

'I recognise the words ...' Miss Isolde appeared from behind the fallen log where she'd been hiding.

Frowning, she tilted her head, trying to listen. 'Those words were in the book, I kept dreaming about them.' She smiled. 'The Fae are chanting: *Chosen.*'

Tingles tumbled through my stomach and I stared at Lloyd. *No, surely not . . . ?*

More Fae sprang forward out of the bushes; these ones looked like woodland creatures, some with four legs, some with feathers and tails and fur. All different, all beautiful, with huge shining eyes, the colour of the sun. Eyes blazing, they swarmed towards the Champion and tore the leaves from his face.

He had both his hands on my sword's hilt. 'Help me!' he ordered, his eyes dark and angry. The Fae linked hands and formed a circle around him. Whispers babbled through them as they looked between each other, nodding and smiling.

'No – what are you—'

They'd heard what he'd said and weren't going to blindly obey him any more.

Smaller Fae, no taller than us, scampered along the ground and clustered inside the circle of bigger Fae, moving even closer to the Champion. Hands clasped tight, they stomped their feet heavily, as if marching on the spot. Their muttering grew louder, and deep splits swelled through the mud, hunks of earth crumbling away as vines writhed and wrapped themselves tightly around the Champion's wrists and ankles.

Suddenly they all burst forward, closing in so tight around the Champion that we could barely see him. There was an enormous crack, louder than thunder, and then the ground fractured and swallowed the Champion back up.

Nat and Lloyd ran over to Miss Isolde. Lloyd carefully untied her hands. She rubbed her wrists, flinching, where the twine had left deep marks.

'Thank you, dear,' she said, looking around her carefully. Triumphant chanting still echoed around us from the bushes. The Fae now stared at us, many of them smiling.

'What if ... what if we *are* the Chosen?' I said quietly.

'Us?' Arlene asked. 'But how?'

The idea grew in my mind: *Lloyd's tracking, my fire, Nat's illusions, Arlene's singing ...*

'Don't you see? Maybe being Chosen isn't just something you *are*, but something you can *become*?'

Arlene and Nat looked at each other and then at Lloyd and me.

'Yes!' Lloyd nodded eagerly. 'We *chose* to come here to help.'

'I think I understand.' Arlene smiled. 'No one else can tell us who we can be, or what we can do.'

'We decided it for ourselves,' Nat said.

We did.

'Maybe that's where true power lies,' Miss Isolde said softly. 'Each of you is special in your own way, but none of you believed it before. But together, you bring out the very best in each other. Working together – you become extraordinary.' She beamed at us, pride and love written all over her face. 'Absolutely magical.'

Chapter Twenty-Two

The End

It was a long and quiet walk back through Fae Feld. With each step we took, our armour fell away. It was bittersweet, watching our silver chainmail dissolve back into the earth. Uphill, we sometimes tripped over loose pebbles, our feet scrabbling to find purchase. But chants of *Chosen, Chosen, Chosen* echoed from every corner, along with tingling bells, drumming, claps and whistles, all unseen. We knew that with the Champion gone, the Feld could return to how it was before he'd come and changed things. Already buds started to quiver open, and huge-winged butterflies lingered on the blooms. The air was filled with noise now: crickets and bees.

Eventually we reached the right path to lead us back to the cairn entrance. Clods of earth started shifting, as they'd done when we first descended underground. We huddled together as we slowly rose, the earth carrying us up into a darkening blue sky.

Reaching the top, Nat and Arlene both hugged Miss Isolde tight, and the five of us stood like that for a while, at the top of the cairn, as our eyes adjusted, seeing the dusk settle around us.

Miss Isolde rubbed at her wrists, wincing. 'How can you ever forgive me, children? I'm sorry that I put you in such danger.' She sniffed, her eyes filling with tears. 'I thought – I thought I was doing the right thing, trying to protect you.'

'Maybe we don't need protecting,' I said gently.

'That's right,' Lloyd said. 'Not in the way you think anyway.'

We stepped forward and saw Pal sat on the ground, surrounded by the children and staff of Fablehouse. We ran over to him, and Nat babbled, 'Oh, Pal! The ground gobbled up the Champion and . . .' He threw his arms around Pal's neck and the rest of his words were lost.

Pal flashed his bright smile at us. 'My brave knights have returned, all in one piece I see.'

I was so happy to see his face again. 'I . . . I wasn't sure if we would—'

'Enough.' He held up his hand to stop my words. 'I never doubted your purity of heart, Roamers. I knew you would prosper.'

As the fresh evening air cleared their heads, everyone gradually came back to their senses.

Pal looked at Miss Isolde, who was standing off to one side. He stood up, extending his arm, and swept it across himself, in a low bow. 'I am greatly honoured to make your acquaintance.' A smile twitched at his lips.

'And I yours,' she replied, bowing her head, her cheeks flushed.

A gust of wind made everyone gasp. Wisps and trails of green smoke rushed across the heathland towards us, thrashing at the stones. We glanced around, watchful.

'Rest easy. The Fae are returning to Fae Feld,' Pal said. 'There isn't much time before the doorway will be sealed up again. We have one more task to do.'

'Destroy the grimoire!' Miss Isolde said.

'You are correct,' Pal said. 'We need to light a fire and burn the book as the sun sets. Then we shall toss the ashes over the cliffs, into the sea, scattered to the four winds.'

'Do we really need to burn it?' I asked, horrified at the idea of destroying something so beautiful and powerful.

'I'm sorry,' Pal said softly, 'but burning is the only way to destroy the malignant magic within.'

'We'll need wood then,' I replied simply.

Nat, Lloyd and Arlene headed over to a line of trees to collect loose twigs and branches. I touched Miss Isolde's sleeve, urging her to one side.

I cleared my throat. 'Can I ask you something, miss?'

She laid her hand gently on top of my head. 'Of course, Heather, dear.'

'What happened exactly – with you and the Fae?'

She gazed upwards and sighed. 'After I discovered those old books, the grimoire began to speak to me, in my dreams. Fablehouse is always on my mind, and one evening, before I knew what I was doing, I found myself at the cairn with the book open in my hands.

The stones shifted, and the Fae promised me that we could all live untroubled by the outside world if I made a bargain with them. They said they could create magic which meant that outsiders would be unable to enter Fablehouse; they swore people would almost forget Fablehouse existed. We would be left in peace.'

Miss Isolde lowered her voice. 'I thought it was the right thing to do, especially for the younger ones . . . They have no idea they don't look the same as everyone else.'

'Do you mean the colour of their skin?' I said.

'Their skin is gorgeous! Each and every one. But they came here so young. I have heard the comments and seen the stares. It hurt my heart, knowing that their lives might always be full of struggle, proving themselves over and over.'

Miss Isolde's smile was sad. 'I wanted to protect them from that for just a little while longer. I didn't want them to be pointed at or teased. You and the others know what it's like to be judged on appearances only.'

My heart softened against her; she'd done the

wrong thing but for the right reasons. 'You're right. It's not fair.'

'But I know now that my duty *isn't* to hide you away. My mission is to ensure that people *do* see you and your true glory and the unique talents you each have. To celebrate and delight in all which makes us different.'

She put her hands on my shoulder and brought me in close to her.

* * *

We sat in a circle around the fire that Pal and Lloyd built. With the sun lowering itself in the sky, a burning fiery-orange ball, Davey yawned, eyes closing. Arlene sang lullabies while Pal tore pages from the grimoire, and one by one, laid them on to the flames.

We watched the pages blacken and curl. One flapped up into the air and whisked itself off over the cliff. Purple and green smoke whistled and rose into the air before dispersing. After the last page was gone, the fire flickered out and the hazy horizon darkened. Fireflies lit up the sky.

'What's next for us?' I asked aloud.

Miss Isolde looked at us and said, 'We aren't hiding away any longer. I shall speak to the council and school inspectors and make it clear to them that separation is not the way forward. You are a part of this society.'

Nat rubbed his eyes before staring into the dying embers. 'And we're here to stay.'

Once the fire had cooled, a deep rumbling underneath us started up. I jolted, frightened that the Champion had somehow returned, that it was him thundering underneath us, but it was the land all around the cairn.

'Oh!' Arlene breathed, pulling on Lloyd's and Nat's sleeves. 'Look!'

The scattered fallen stones began to quiver, and then they moved, sliding along the ground. Stones began to stack up, reassembling themselves. We sat back, amazed, as the stones, all shapes and sizes, rebuilt themselves into the cairn once again.

'The Stony Tower!' Nat crowed.

'Do you have to go back to sleep again?' I asked Pal, hoping he'd say no. I wasn't sure we could bear for him to leave us. He'd been a part of us always, or so it seemed.

'I shan't return to slumber this time,' Pal said. 'History has been forever changed. I shall remain in this realm. I hope that my own power exists within me, but I do not yet understand what that may be. It's a long journey ahead – discovering not only where I should go next, but also ... where I've been.'

'Maybe you could do that by ... staying here?' Lloyd suggested, looking towards Miss Isolde hopefully. Nat's eyes lit up.

'Oh yes, stay with us!' Arlene added.

'If Pal chooses Fablehouse as his home,' Miss Isolde said warmly, 'he is welcome to live with us.'

'Yay!' Nat said. He leaped up and ran round the circle. 'Pal's staying!'

Pal smiled, and I saw the tears in his eyes, the tiger-orange embers reflected in them. He lowered his head, his hair ropes swinging, and said, 'I can be of use; there are many tasks I can do.'

'You don't need to *do* anything,' Lloyd said, laying a hand on Pal's arm. 'You don't need to prove your worth. You're one of us, you can just ... *be*.'

Pal offered his hand and helped Miss Isolde up. Guided by the stars just making themselves known above us, the two of them headed back, with the others, across the moors.

'Fablehouse is very special, isn't it?' Arlene said, linking her fingers through mine. 'We need to protect it always.'

'Roamers forever,' Lloyd said.

Nat beamed at us. 'Nothing will ever break us apart.'

We smiled at one another, stood there on our moorland, the dusk folding itself around us like a blanket. Rich sounds of the night trilled: owls and the last birdsong, badgers and rabbits snuffling and squeaking. Together, we had saved our land, and now it was settling down to sleep.

'It's time to go,' I said.

Finally, I'd found where I belonged.

I was on my way home.

Author's Note

The idea of *Fablehouse* – a story about four children finding a Black Arthurian Knight who helps them defeat the Fae intent on taking over their world – was instantly appealing and exciting to me. What's interesting, though, is that often, as a writer, even if I *think* I'm writing about one thing, sometimes, after a while, it becomes clear that I'm *really* writing about something else. And that was definitely the case with this story.

As I wrote, and the story developed, I realised that *Fablehouse* couldn't help but contain and reflect my childhood feelings, experiences and worries from when I was growing up, living in residential children's homes and foster placements.

My childhood was fractured and scary: I hid under beds to avoid raised voices. I lined up, hoping to be chosen by prospective foster parents. I learned that I would never be the 'right sort' – too loud, too brown, not enough. Drawing attention to myself wasn't wise and was often dangerous. So I always felt that I belonged everywhere and nowhere. I'm an inhabitant of multiple worlds and identities: mixed-race, Welsh, Jewish. Never quite accepted or acceptable.

But when I sat down to write the first scene, Heather's voice immediately sprang to life as I, in part at least, transformed into my younger self. I recognised exactly how hurt and defensive Heather felt at the beginning of the story, because that had been me. I understood how isolated these different children felt, separated from their fathers, and how they'd feel about Pal – because that had been me too. I knew precisely how important and special their cairn was, because, although I didn't grow up in one place, I loved exploring whichever new village, town or city I found myself in. I always found some piece of land to connect with.

With no brothers or sisters, I created my own 'roamers': a group of imaginary friends who I took with me on my adventures. I'd go on ten-mile bike rides to the local cinema (where my obsession with *Empire of the Sun* meant I saw it more than ten times) and became fascinated by 1940s and 1950s Hollywood, just like Arlene. At one point I was interested in magic and used to put on little magic shows, just like Nat. I played chess and read books all the time, like Lloyd, losing myself in happier worlds. I was always searching for connection – just like Heather.

Fablehouse is based on a real place that you can visit – Holnicote House – which was a Somerset orphanage and once home to the 'Brown Babies' of white women and Black American GIs. I went on a walking holiday to Exmoor to research *Fablehouse* and felt an immediate connection with the characters in my story and the world and landscape in which they lived and explored.

Telling stories to you is how I find connection now, and writing remains my greatest source of joy and comfort. I hope that you've enjoyed reading about Heather and the Roamers as much as I have enjoyed writing about them.

With love.

Bonus Chapter
The Truest Quest

The midnight sky over Exmoor is vast and black and sprinkled with stars. It's a few weeks after Fae Feld, and Pal, Miss Isolde and us Roamers are camping overnight on the moors.

Pal has moved into the old caretaker's cottage at the bottom of the Fablehouse garden, but he claims he tosses and turns most nights, unused to such a small space. His eyes misted over when he said how he longs for the wild, the freedom, the nip of the crisp morning air so, to cheer him up, Miss Isolde suggested that we had a mini adventure sleeping under the stars.

Now, Miss Isolde pours tea from a flask and passes us all a tin mug.

'It still astounds me – how man can control and create fire,' Pal says, adjusting the large stones that he's placed in a ring. 'These stones will keep our fire safe and contained; essential so that no one gets hurt.'

He moves around now, poking at the burning twigs with a stick. Clumps of moss and dried leaves sizzle and crackle as they catch alight.

I lay propped up on my elbows. My heart soars seeing pinpricks of brightness illuminate the dark sky. My mum told me once that there was always light to be found, even during the blackest of nights – and she was right. According to Lloyd, the stars we see actually died a long time ago, yet still they throw out their afterglow for us.

'Isn't it beautiful?' Arlene shuffles closer so that our knees and shoulders are touching, connecting.

'Magical,' I reply.

Arlene and I have become as close as I imagine sisters might be. Each night, she sings to me, and I'm amazed by how she never forgets the words to any song. I asked, 'But how do you remember them all?' and she laughed and pointed to her heart. 'They're all kept here,' she said. 'Every time it beats, a tune bursts alive in me.'

Whenever she sings, it's as if the cracks in my own heart heal a little. It feels less . . . fragile.

Now, as Pal sits back down – his face calm and eyes gazing into the sparking flames – Nat, hugging his knees, looks over at him.

'Pal,' he says. 'Can you tell us about when you were a boy?'

We all turn to Pal, waiting. We know so little about this brave knight who we found beaten and broken at the cairn. We'd heard of the myths and legends, of course – who hadn't? – maidens rescued and beasts slain, as was a knight's duty. But what about the things he'd never spoken of; the things left out of the books?

'Yes, tell us a story,' urged Lloyd.

Lloyd sits opposite me and I glance across the fire at him, every part of me flooding with gladness that he'd been by my side battling the Champion. We'd made the perfect team.

Pal sweeps his thick hair ropes round his shoulder, tying them up with an emerald-green sash. He looks around the fire – his dark eyes taking us in, one by one. Not shy to let his gaze linger on our faces, seeing us for who we really are. It's quite something – being seen like that.

'I am one of three sons, and my father was King Astlabor.' He focuses on the fire and fixes his eyes on a hunk of wood which, as it crumbles and burns away, changes shape, quivering with orange sparks which whisk into the wind. Pal watches the dying grey ash float away into the night.

'Which stories reveal who a man truly is? What tales demonstrate where he comes from, where he is going and who he's been? The annals of time cause me to forget many instances – seasons converge and confuse in my mind, constant and yet ever-changing, like the waves breaking upon the shore.'

'But I bet there's them things like big battles and feasts that you never forget, right?' says Nat, eyes hungry for tales of glory.

Pal laughs a little and places his huge hand on top of Nat's curls, squashing them flat.

'Indeed, young Nathaniel ... indeed.'

'Well ... tell us any story then,' I say. 'Whatever comes to mind, Sir Palamedes ...'

Something happens then, a charge rushes through the air – sparked by me using his full name, perhaps – because he sits up straighter and his eyes flare with a sudden gleam. The flames reflected there dance and weave as I imagine he did in battle, astride his horse.

'There was a woman whom I loved with every fibre of my being.'

'What happened?' whispers Miss Isolde, leaning forward, hands clamped around her tin mug, cheeks pink from the steam.

'Alas –' Pal's eyes dull – 'it was not to be. Even though her parents favoured me – she only had eyes for Tristan. He and I fought many times, and I parried well, but each time he won he made me swear to forsake Lady Isolde.'

'And did you?' breathes Arlene.

'I had to. A knight's word is his bond. Your honour and word are precious, even if you have nothing else to your name. My love never waned; I was consumed with longing. But, knowing it was not to be, I tried to devote my life to gallant acts instead – though most left me hollow and unfulfilled. I was searching for that which would fill me with purpose and belonging.'

Pal fell silent then. We all stared into the fire. The wood blazed red and orange and blue, and silhouettes flickered to life in the crumbling, crackling splinters.

'I made many errors of judgement as a young knight.' Pal shook his head.

'But you're a hero!' exclaims Nat.

A small smile curls at Pal's lips. 'I consider myself a knight first and foremost, but I am a man too and it is vital to understand that we are ... fallible creatures.'

'Falli-*what*?' asks Arlene, wrinkling her nose.

'Falli*ble*. It means capable of being wrong,' Miss Isolde chimes in. 'Everyone can make mistakes.'

'So no one's perfect?' I ask, looking at her.

'That's right, Heather. Making mistakes, or even sometimes doing the wrong thing, doesn't matter. What counts is how you take responsibility for your part in any wrongdoing.'

Here she falls silent, and I know she must be remembering her decision to bargain with the Fae.

'I felt I had so much to prove,' Pal carries on. 'So I fought and fought, full of fire and fear, and even though many named me valiant, whatever I did and wherever I turned, Tristan always overshadowed me.'

His shoulders suddenly sag, and my eyes prickle with tears. I can't bear it – there was no knight better or braver than our Pal.

'Well, you're the only one still standing!' Nat burst out, clearly feeling the same.

'So what did you do?' Lloyd blows across the top of his mug, watching Pal keenly.

'I rescued Lady Isolde's favourite handmaid, Dame Bragwaine, from a tree and hoped Isolde would see me in a good light. She did agree to come away with me, but we were pursued. Actually, I have Isolde to thank for my appointment at King Arthur's court. And it was there, finally, that I put aside thoughts of love and instead turned to devoting myself to Arthur's service. After King Pellinore told us about a monstrous questing beast, the idea to hunt it down appeared in my mind.'

'But if it was so dangerous, why go after it?' Lloyd asks.

'I needed a distraction from my broken heart,' Pal says simply. 'If I could not devote myself to love, I needed to devote myself to a nobler cause. Perhaps I knew slaying the beast would prove impossible, but sometimes the making of a man is ... in the striving. And I strived harder than anyone.'

'Why did you try so hard?' I ask.

Pal's eyes crinkle at the corners, but his smile is sad. 'I was always both insider and outsider, never one nor the other. I was so weary, always trying to find a place to belong.'

Lloyd and I smile at each other; we know what that means, how that feels.

'The love stuff is a bit ... mushy,' Nat says. 'But tell us about your boss, King Arthur.'

'Arthur crushed the Saxons and became a hero.'

'Did you live in a castle?'

'Oh yes. The castle in Camelot had a round table, the idea of which meant no one was more important than anyone else, although, of course, some knights felt they were special. But in principle, the round table was a fair idea.'

'Was the castle very grand?' sighs Arlene, hands

folded under her chin, a faraway look on her face, no doubt thinking of princesses and their fancy gowns and jewels.

'It was magnificent. We had a moat! And a good set-up for defences. Often we stood on the barbican – a defensive tower – at the entrance. An excellent place for hurling stones at the enemy, although if you could reach them from there, they were already too close.'

Miss Isolde coughs. 'Palamedes,' her voice a little stern. 'I do *not* want these children's heads filled with bloody images of death and destruction.'

'But you did not wish to hear tales of love either!' He spreads his palms wide and chuckles. 'Then I am at a loss. My entire existence thus far has consisted of fighting, feasting and ... pining after Isolde. What else is a man's life?'

Miss Isolde looks as if she's trying to swallow a laugh and clears her throat.

'Well, I for one would love to hear about a medieval feast! The war rationing has given me quite the appetite. Tell us, what were your favourite foods?'

Pal's eyes grow misty in memory. 'Oh! King Arthur's feasts were legendary! Landowners grew their own food and we prayed for good weather so that we might not go hungry. My favourite was boar, of course, but frumenty was most delicious!'

'What's that?' I ask.

Pal frowns, thinking how best to describe it. 'Hmm, you'd most likely consider it similar to porridge.'

'Eww!' says Nat, poking out his tongue.

'Ah, but with the right spices it really is a warming dish,' Pal says. He puts his fingers to his lips, tapping gently. 'What else? Imagine if you will, a long table heaving with food: game and pies and soup and chicken. Golden goblets, and candlesticks which towered over everyone, throwing out delicate light. We'd eat seven or eight different meat dishes and drink from pewter tankards overflowing with mead, ale, cider ... 'Tis making my mouth fair water just thinking of those days! Then there were dances and entertainment, with people telling stories.

'Camelot was a city surrounded by green forests and meadows, lush hills and flowing waters, magical names singing out across time and place, like an incantation from Merlin himself: the Holy Grail, the Temple of the Stars at Glastonbury, Excalibur. Oh, that land held so much for me, *of* me. This is why I feel at peace here on these moors. The area we had for our tournaments was very much like this.'

'I'd love to hear about a tournament!' Lloyd says, eyes shining. 'What was it like?'

'Ah, well. Wooden stands were constructed and set up so that the ladies could watch us fight one another. We were keen to impress, of course.'

'Yay! The good stuff. I wanna hear about swords and slaying dragons!' Nat's eyes light up in excitement.

'Well then, young Nat, let me tell you a tale that will set your heart aflutter. The day the Green Knight galloped into court.'

'The Green Knight?'

'Aye. A gigantic man who towered over everyone. Everything about him was a deep, rich, mossy green: his skin and hair and beard; his horse, and even the axe he carried – a bright, brilliant, blinding green!'

'Really?' I say. 'How can that be true?'

'Powerful sorcery, though we only discovered that later. What do you know of King Arthur's court?'

We fall over ourselves to tell him the stories we know from the Dead Arthur book Miss Isolde gave me.

'Miss Clara read to us about the Sword in the Stone!'

Arlene sets down her tin mug. 'And of course the great love of Lancelot and Guinevere.'

Pal guffaws at our enthusiasm and holds up his hands. 'But not the Green Knight?'

We look at each other and shake our heads. 'Nope,' we chorus.

'Ahhh,' Pal says, cupping his chin, thinking. 'That is a tale indeed. Although you will find no mention of me in any recounting of it.'

'Why not?' I ask.

'It is not for the likes of me to choose who is remembered throughout the ages,' Pal says gravely. 'But if you would like to bear witness to the truth about what happened, then it would be my knight's honour to tell you.'

'Is there blood and guts?' asks Nat, thrilled.

'Yes,' Pal nods. 'I am afraid so.'

'Great!' Nat snuggles down and rearranges the blanket covering his knees.

Miss Isolde chuckles. 'Fine. But, Pal, do keep the gory details to a minimum, please. We don't need any nightmares.'

The hoot from an owl echoes through the night air.

'I shall do my best,' Pal says. 'Although I cannot guarantee anything, because this is a tale of a head chopped off; a head that rolls across a floor of its own accord. I shall begin . . .

'Another year had ended, and Camelot looked magical – tree boughs weighed down with soft white snow. At New Year we feasted; a merry time with more food and drink than any man could wish for. Arthur requested we entertain him with tales of adventure, but before one story left anyone's lips, a great thundering was heard echoing through the castle corridors. Morgan le Fay and I looked at each other, aghast. Then into the court hall roared a huge green stallion with a man astride it. Gasps and whispers flew around the court. "Look at his . . . *skin!*" people cried. "What a beast!"

'The stallion reared up in front of Arthur, its gigantic hoofs glittering green. We drew our swords, on guard to protect and defend, but Arthur demanded the man speak. I recognised how the other knights' eyes roamed fearfully over him, for I'd once felt their eyes on me like that too. This man did not look like anyone they had ever seen. But I was intrigued to see another as foreign as I, and not even slightly afraid.

'Everything about him was as green as the forests. I thought it a trick of the light at first, or one of Merlin's magical creations. In one hand he brandished a glinting green axe and in the other a spray of holly. His voice was lush and dusky as he suggested a beheading game which none of us had heard of nor frankly wanted to play. It did not sound a game to be won! He offered his axe as reward if someone agreed an attempt to behead him. Then he said the most curious thing – that he would return the blow in a year and a day.

'Arthur had been drinking much mead and he

leaped up to fight, but Gawain – Arthur's nephew and the youngest of us all – beat him to it. Before we blinked, Gawain's sword swiped through the air, aimed at the knight's neck. Gawain struck, and with one swift swipe the Green Knight's head cleaved clean off! It rolled across the floor . . . coming to rest next to its headless body. Eyes bigger and shinier than any emeralds stared up at us.'

'I said *no gore!*' Miss Isolde gasps, putting her hand to her mouth.

'And I am true to my word,' Pal says slightly mischievously. 'I have not mentioned blood or guts or . . .'

'Enough – *enough!*' Miss Isolde says. 'Keep the scary details to a minimum please, or we'll resort to singing nursery rhymes instead.'

Pal continued with his tale. 'Then the Green Knight's body picked up his *own head* and the mouth flapped open like a hinge. "In a year and a day, come to find me at court," said the severed head. "My turn to chop *your* head off! Mark my words." And off he went!'

'And then what?' Nat and Lloyd ask together

breathlessly. Arlene and I squeeze hands, unable to take our eyes off Pal.

He snaps branches at his feet and carefully adds them to the fire, which is dying down. Miss Isolde opens a box full of rock buns and passes them round.

'Well, as you can imagine, poor Gawain thought of little else apart from his head being chopped off for the whole year.'

'Well, you would, wouldn't you?!' exclaims Arlene. 'Imagine!'

'He was inexperienced and arrogant, always seeking to gain favour with Arthur, but through the change of seasons, and many other quests and adventures, it played on his mind. He was quite the changed man.'

'Sounds a bit daft,' Lloyd protests. 'Gawain didn't have to go! Who'd ever know?'

'The Green Knight would have come back looking for him, out for his blood!' Nat cries.

'It was more a question of honour – a knight's most valuable commodity.' Pal sounds thoughtful. 'If Gawain did *not* seek out the Green Knight, yes, he might well keep his life, but he would have no honour – nor would the court – and his life would be meaningless. When the time came, Gawain rode off on his steed, Gringolet. But before he set off, Arthur took me aside and told me to follow Gawain at a distance. Arthur was very fond of his nephew and did not wish him to come to any harm. I was tasked with staying in the shadows, but to protect Gawain at all costs.

'And I stayed true to my word. Through many weeks of trials and battles, I made sure Gawain never saw me. Even from a distance, I saved his life on many an occasion.'

'Did you fight dragons?' gulps Nat.

Pal nods. 'Aye, that I did. And they were fearsome and loathsome and scaly and scary. Gawain nearly got overthrown by bandits many times. Without him noticing, I had to throw up distractions; make him think he was committing feats of bravery and daring. He did not realise that it was I who ensured he remained unharmed. He must have thought himself charmed!

'The time of year was bitterly cold, with ice and

hard terrain as far as the eye could see, and I often feared for my horse's life. Gawain stayed a while in a castle, and during those freezing dark nights I considered returning to Camelot. But eventually, on the third day, dawn broke over the snowy silent hills and Gawain emerged. This was the day the Green Knight had specified. I followed Gawain until he came to a dank marshy green.

'And there stood the Green Knight, an axe shining at his side, as powerful and magnificently monstrous as I remembered. Gawain climbed down off Gringolet and tied him to a tree, his hands trembling. His horse whinnied as if he sensed his master's fate as he walked away.

'The Green Knight roared, sounding like a hundred howling, questing beasts. He gestured with his mammoth arms, and I swear everything around us stilled before my very eyes. A falcon froze in mid-air. The Green Knight had stopped time itself. He whirled around, calling out, "You! The dusky one who skulks in the shadows – reveal yourself!" I scarcely believed it, but he pointed at the trees which I hid behind. "Come now, for I shall not wake this world until I bear witness to the most chivalrous of knights. You claim no glory and yet you fight with a warrior's heart!" he bellowed.

'I dismounted and strode forward. I was not afraid of this ginormous man for, as I stepped closer, I saw his expression was wise but impish. As I took in his glowing green skin, and he took in my black, a gentle understanding passed between us.

'"You are as dark and mysterious as the night," he said. "I've watched you protecting that foolhardy boy. Why?"

'"It is my quest," I explained.

'He laughed heartily. "You deserve a better quest than chasing an upstart around the winter countryside!"

'We stared at one another for a long, silent while. I wondered if he meant to chop *my* head off. But then he sighed and, as he did so, a green mist fluttered from his lips and his shoulders slumped.

'"Be like the brook: let everything flow around you. Do not resist, nor get dragged under. Then, and only then, can your true quest find you," he whispered, looking tired and worn. "I read ripples of concern in your creased brow, but never doubt that you are needed. Now – hide among the trees again while I bid this young knight well and offer him a lesson."

'With a flourish of his fingers, the Green Knight released time back into the world and he and Gawain took up their bargain.

'And afterwards, off I dashed, the frozen ground yielding under my horse's hoofs. His whispered words often come back to me, sometimes at the oddest times, and I can almost feel his breath on my cheek and in my ears.'

Pal leans forward and softly blows on to the fire, coaxing dying embers back to life. He unties the emerald-green sash, letting his hair ropes fall free. The firelight illuminates his strong, square jawline and broad, noble forehead. I am transfixed by his *radiant, beautiful skin.* 'And the Green Knight was right, wasn't he?' I say, grinning.

Pal raises an eyebrow.

Lloyd catches my eye, reading my mind. 'Your true quest *did* find you,' he adds.

'*We* found you,' Arlene and Nat say together.

Miss Isolde shifts closer to Pal, linking arms. Her hand rests lightly on top of his. 'And *you* found us.'

'In my pain, I have indeed found purpose,' Pal murmurs. 'Purpose and pleasure.'

I lay back, letting my gaze drift across the inky-black sky, taking in the wonder of the silver-white pinpricks of faraway light.

Out there is the whole world. A whole world just waiting; waiting for all of us to find our truest quest.

Look for the symbol at the start of each chapter,
crack the code and unlock a secret *Fablehouse* message . . .

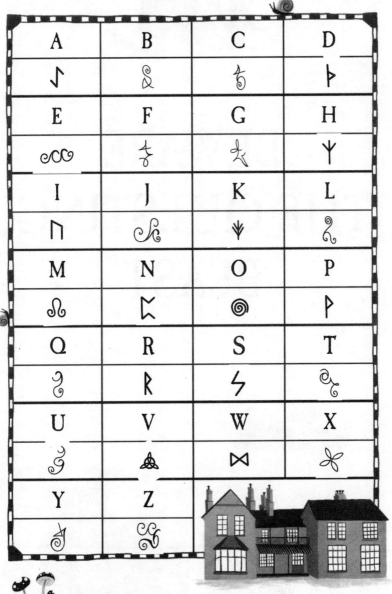

Turn the page to reveal the answer . . .

BEWARE
THE QUESTING
BEAST

Enjoyed *Fablehouse* and want to find out more about the history and themes in the book? Here are some interesting resources and websites you could use to go beyond *Fablehouse* ...

Become

becomecharity.org.uk

Become's mission is to help children in care and young care leavers to believe in themselves and to heal, grow and unleash their potential. The charity works alongside these young people to make the care system the best it can be.

Care Experienced History Month

careexperiencedhistorymonth.org

Care Experienced people have been a part of societies across the world for as long as can be remembered. Care Experienced History Month takes place in April each year and calls for global recognition of this history.

Mixed Museum

mixedmuseum.org.uk

The Mixed Museum is a digital museum and archive seeking to preserve and share the history of racial mixing in Britain for future generations as part of its contribution to the widening of knowledge about the Black and Asian and wider ethnic minority presence in Britain.

Comfort Cases UK

comfortcasesuk.org

No child should ever have to carry their life in a bin bag. Comfort Cases UK's mission is to bring a sense of hope and dignity to children moving around the UK foster care system by ending this practice and giving these children an unbranded backpack filled with items centred around their needs and showing them they are loved and respected (a comfort case).

Madlug

madlug.com

Madlug was founded in 2015 by Dave Linton when he learned that most children in care have their belongings moved in a bin bag. He started Madlug and came up with a 'Buy one, Wear one, Help one' approach – with every bag purchased, a pack-away travel bag goes to a child in care.

There have also been some interesting films and podcasts produced about the history of Britain's 'Brown Babies', two of which are as follows:

BBC World Service: Witness History: Britain's World War Two 'Brown Babies'
bbc.co.uk/programmes/w3csywvr

BBC World Service podcast: WW2 'Brown Babies': A little-known part of British 20th Century history
youtube.com/watch?v=oi4Ll7VGXJk

Acknowledgements

Fablehouse wouldn't exist without Jasmine Richards's company, Storymix, which is dedicated to ensuring that *all* children can see themselves as the hero. Jasmine read a book called *Britain's 'Brown Babies'* by Lucy Bland, and then, knowing my background of growing up in children's and foster homes, approached me with her idea: four children finding a Black knight. Thank you, Jasmine, for your ideas, enthusiasm and support – and for trusting my storytelling instincts!

Books are a collaboration, and when Jasmine mentioned Fablehouse, a favourite (old) film came to mind – *Whistle Down the Wind*. Heather came to me immediately, her voice strong and loud.

Thanks to my agent, Philippa Milnes-Smith at The Soho Agency, for always doing the very best for me.

Thank you to Thy Bui for a cover and maps to slay champions over and to Lola Idowu for the fabulous illustrations!

Thanks to all at Bloomsbury – Fliss Stevens, Hannah Sandford, Kathy Webb, Alex Antscherl, Beatrice Cross and the entire team who are bringing *Fablehouse* into the world. Everyone has welcomed me into the Bloomsbury family. I'm so proud to have them publish *Fablehouse*.

Biggest thanks and rib-crushing hugs go to my editor, Zöe Griffiths. Not only is she wonderful company, with fantastic taste in food and TV, but she championed this book and my writing from the beginning. She bowled me over with her passion and has led me gently through this entire process, quietly but confidently, always letting me know that she believed in me, even when I often doubted myself.

Thank you to all librarians – without you I would never have discovered my love of reading.

Thank you to English teachers everywhere. I had two amazing ones – Mrs Hughes and Mr Poole. I'll never forget them.

Samuel and Maisy – my roamers. Watching you become who you are is a gift.

And for Ed, who, from the first time I laid eyes on him in 1997, has always made me feel that I'm safe and that I'm ... *home*.

Don't miss
the stunning sequel to

Can Heather and the Roamers stay together, be accepted
and discover their true destinies?

Coming April 2024

About the Author

Emma Norry has a BA (Hons) in Film and an MA in Screenwriting. Emma's previous books include *Son of the Circus*, which was shortlisted for the Diverse Book Awards, *Amber Under Cover*, a middle-grade adventure about a teenage spy, *The Extraordinary Life of Nelson Mandela* and *Football Legends: Lionel Messi*. Her short stories have been published in the anthologies *The Very Merry Murder Club*, *Happy Here: 10 stories from Black British authors and illustrators*, *The Place for Me: Stories about the Windrush Generation* and *Home Again: Stories about Coming Home from War*. *Fablehouse* is Emma's first book for Bloomsbury.

Emma grew up in the care system in Cardiff, Wales. She now lives and works in Bournemouth with her husband and family.